LETTERS TO MY
FATHER

CRISSIE ANN LEONARD

WESTBOW
PRESS®
A DIVISION OF THOMAS NELSON
& ZONDERVAN

WestBow Press books may be ordered through booksellers or by contacting:

WestBow Press
A Division of Thomas Nelson & Zondervan
1663 Liberty Drive
Bloomington, IN 47403
www.westbowpress.com
1 (866) 928-1240

THE HOLY BIBLE, NEW INTERNATIONAL VERSION®, NIV® Copyright © 1973, 1978, 1984, 2011 by Biblica, Inc.® Used by permission. All rights reserved worldwide.

ISBN: 978-1-9736-7509-9 (sc)
ISBN: 978-1-9736-7510-5 (hc)
ISBN: 978-1-9736-7508-2 (e)

Library of Congress Control Number: 2019914495

Print information available on the last page.

WestBow Press rev. date: 09/25/2019

To anyone who has ever asked God a question and struggled to find peace in the answer

Surround yourself with the dreamers and the doers, the believers and the thinkers, but most of all, surround yourself with those who see the greatness within you, even when you don't see it yourself.

—Edmund Lee, author

Contents

Acknowledgments

First and foremost, I want to thank God for saving me. His purpose met my pain, and he gave me the strength and courage to chase my dream. God showed me that he was bigger than any doubts I had about being worthy of that dream.

I want to thank my mom, Kathie. She taught me that sometimes you must sacrifice in order to chase your dream, but the dream worth chasing is worth the sacrifice.

I want to thank my sister, Carrie, and her husband, Gino. They taught me to never give up on your dream, no matter how long it takes you to achieve it.

I want to thank my friend, Anne Pirhalla. She taught me to believe in myself, even when the obstacles seem impossible to overcome.

I want to thank my best friends, Meghan Roll and Marilyn Howard, for taking time out of their lives to help me achieve my dream. They believed in me when I didn't believe in myself. They saw the oak tree where I only saw the acorn. Without them, this book would never have happened.

Last, I want to thank my church, Simple Church, in Reynoldsburg, Ohio. They gave me a place to call home. Through their teachings and friendships, I discovered my purpose and found the confidence to finish this book.

Prologue

Sandbridge Beach, Sandbridge, Virginia
May 25, 2015

My name is Wiletta Jayne. I'm a forty-three-year-old, peace-and-tranquility beach-lover, trapped inside a city girl. I've always taken pride in having a strong relationship with God, my heavenly Father. It was the one constant in my life. We talked daily, and I felt safe in his arms and surrounded by his love.

Lately, my chaotic lifestyle has monopolized my life, to the point that I no longer have time to nurture that relationship. Now, I feel lonely and lost. My drive and passion have dimmed, but mostly I miss his presence in my life.

I longed to hear his voice again, so I took some time off work, with the intent of devoting more time to him. I told him how much I missed him and that I hoped he would meet me at the beach in a few days. I loaded my car, put the top down, and started out on my journey to the beach. I knew the feel of the sun on my face, sand in my toes, and the privacy and quietness of the beach was just what I needed.

I was singing along with my favorite songs, about halfway

to the beach, when I felt a sudden urge to take the exit I saw up ahead of me. As I neared the exit, the urge grew stronger. I knew something important must be there, so I turned onto the exit. As I sat at the stop sign at the end of the exit road, I wondered which way to go. Then I saw it—a small garage-sale sign. I smiled, recalling memories of my best friend, Faith, and me, driving around, looking for these signs.

I drove a mile or so until I found the sale. As I approached it, trying to decide where to begin, a small table in the back caught my eye—and I knew with absolute certainty that the stack of letters on the corner of the table was meant for me.

No one there seemed to know where they'd come from, but I was drawn to them. I purchased the letters and a small basket to carry them and started back on the road to the beach. Throughout the remainder of the drive, I kept glancing at the letters, wondering what purpose they had on my journey. I made it to the beach house, unpacked the car, ate some dinner, and fell into a deep, restful sleep.

Chapter 1

THE LETTERS

I awoke the next morning to a familiar voice saying, "Good morning, daughter. I see you found the letters."

Relief and affirmation filled me. My Father did meet me here at the beach house, and the letters were meant for me to find. I quickly dressed and had breakfast—eggs, bacon, and a steaming cup of tea. Then, picking up the basket, I went out onto the back porch.

The rocker I sat in faced the ocean. The sun was up, the sky empty of clouds, and for a few minutes, I simply rocked and enjoyed the sound of the waves and seagulls. Closing my eyes, my prayer was simple: "Thank you."

I turned my attention to the basket on the stool next to me. With butterflies in my stomach, I opened the top letter and found it was printed on lined grade-school paper.

> Hi, I'm Joseph, and my mom and I need some help. My mom works all the time. I know she needs to work so we can live in our apartment and have food on our table, but I miss her. I'm only

seven and am too young to work to help Mom pay the bills.

Can you send some help to my mom so I can see her more?

Could you send me a friend so I won't be so lonely?

Joseph

I carefully refolded Joseph's letter and placed it in its envelope.

The next letter was written on cheap stationery. The script was a tiny scrawl and difficult to read.

Why have you done this to me again? This is the fourth time! I just want someone to love, to give the joy I never knew as a child!

Do you know the pain and anger I feel? Eight months this time. I felt her move, heard her heartbeat, saw her little body. I did everything right: ate properly, rested, and took my vitamins. I felt such joy, reading to her and singing lullabies. Why did you take her? Why don't I deserve a child? Is my past so unforgivable?

My husband tells me to lean into you and let your love help me. He prays nightly for peace, yet I know I will never find it. I don't feel love for you, only contempt! Because of you, I only feel grief and emptiness, not joy and completeness. I don't care if I ever hear from you again!

A pink dress, bonnet, and shoes that she will
never wear because of you!

Katerina

My hands were trembling as I put Katerina's letter back in
its envelope. Her grief and anger broke my heart. I pushed gently
with my feet and matched my rocker to the steady rhythm of the
waves coming ashore, letting both soothe me.

I closed my eyes as I reached for the next letter. "Father, are
they all like these first two?" I opened it to find typed words on
pink stationery with hearts in the corners. I smiled and read:

How did it feel to be a daddy's girl? It was the
greatest feeling in the world. My dad was my hero,
my friend, and the first man to capture my heart.

I was his "mini-me." I woke up early every
morning to talk to him. I strived for greatness in
school, so he would be proud. I aspired to follow
in his footsteps and join the military when I was
older. I loved traveling with him or just spending
time together on the couch. Those nine years were
great and so full of love and joy. I thought my
heart would burst from all the love. The sun and
moon rose with my dad, and my life was perfect.

Then I turned ten, and my perfect life fell apart.
That was the year my dad left. The man who once
held my heart had shattered it. There would be no
more daddy-daughter days at school, no father-
daughter dances in the future, no more Daddy

playing Santa Claus at Christmas, and above all, there would be no more Daddy in my life.

A part of that fun, loving, and ambitious little girl died that day. My once full and loving heart knew only sadness and pain. The man I loved, trusted, and expected to be with me always had abandoned me. I never imagined how much the trauma of that loss would affect my life.

As the years passed, I tried to fill the void. I looked for love in all the wrong places. I always searched for the next best thing instead of appreciating what I already had. My bad habits became self-destructive behaviors, which made it hard to trust anyone. I have found it hard to fully open my heart to others for fear of the heartache that may follow.

I try desperately to control who enters my life, hoping to avoid the agonizing pain of abandonment again. Somehow, they always leave, and then those old familiar feelings fill the holes created by their absence. I start to go through the whys in my head: Why did they leave? Why am I not good enough to be their friend? Why doesn't anyone love me? Why can't anyone be a steady figure in my life? And finally, the big question—what could I have done differently to make them stay?

Why is it so easy to believe that, in the end,
they will all leave me? More important, why do I
always think the defect is in me instead of them?

Father, why is my life like this? What do you
do when the first man you ever loved broke your
heart beyond repair?

Cristina

I finished Cristina's letter, thankful for my own father. I
felt tired and drained, so I went inside to take a quick nap. The
comfort and warmth of my Father's presence and the sound of
the ocean tide lulled me to sleep.

A late-afternoon sun greeted me when I awoke. That was not
the quick nap I'd intended, but I felt so refreshed. I must have
needed the rest. I returned to my rocker, carrying the basket of
letters and my prayer journal. I had two more letters to read, but
I found myself reaching for the first three. Holding them close to
my heart with one hand, I opened my journal and began writing:

Thank you, Father, for this time of rest. I am so
grateful that you are here with me. I've spent too
much time away from you, and for that, I am so
sorry. Help me understand the letters. Am I to do
something other than read them? For now, Father,
I offer my prayers for your children. I know you
love each of them.

I pray you watch over Joseph as he struggles
with his mom's prolonged absence for work. I

5

ask that you provide some type of relief for his mother, so she doesn't miss out on her son's life. I pray you find it in your heart to provide Joseph with a companion, so he has someone to spend time with while his mother works to provide him with a better life.

Father, Katerina has felt the grief of a tremendous loss, not once, not twice, but four times. Many would not be able to recover—to feel love again. I pray that Katerina does not become one of those people, Father. I pray that even during her grief and anger, you shower her with your love and grace. We don't know why these terrible things happen to us, but I pray that your plan for Katerina is so much greater than these terrible tragedies. I pray she never hardens her heart against love and that, in time, you will help her to heal and know love again. I pray that somewhere there is a child waiting to call Katerina his or her mom.

May Katerina find the strength to carry on, so she can someday meet this child.

Father, one of the worst feelings in the world is feeling all alone. I pray you surround Cristina with your love until the one thing she knows for sure is your presence. I pray, in her time of need, that she calls out to you, to shine light onto her darkest times. I pray your presence in her life will give her hope for better and brighter days to come.

Wiletta

The next morning, after a long walk along the beach, I returned to my rocker with the basket of letters. I was curious what petitions to God I would read in the final two letters.

The first one, like Cristina's, was typed.

You let all this happen to me. Why couldn't you change me?

For many years, food was an afterthought for me. Food sustained my body and allowed me to enjoy life to its fullest. I enjoyed spending time with family and friends, traveling with my wife, reading a book, and even just sitting outside. Then everything changed.

I remember that day clearly. I got home from work, and my wife said, "We need to talk." Immediately, my defenses went up. I prepared for the worst while hoping for the best. Turns out the worst was in store for me on that day. My wife told me she had fallen out of love with me and wanted a divorce. She spoke of the many reasons why she felt this way and that she wished things could be different. I saw her lips moving, but I barely heard half of what she said, because I was still stuck on the "I want a divorce" part. She left that night. I sat and recalled our life together, while trying to figure out what I had done wrong and what I could have changed to make her stay. I cried the night away over pizza and beer.

I spent the nights leading up to the divorce hearing in the same pattern. Each night I would order a pizza or grab takeout food and sit and think of what I could have done differently. When the pain of my loss and broken heart became too much to bear, I would watch TV or rent a movie to distract myself. Snacking was a part of the distraction, and I always found my hand inside a chip or cookie bag. I told myself it was okay because I was grieving.

Divorce day arrived. I was a wreck as I walked out of the courthouse. She looked like a million dollars, like she'd really taken care of herself while waiting to be free of me. I resented her for, obviously, not caring. I decided to take myself out to dinner to celebrate my having made it through this day and for keeping my composure during the proceedings. I hated her, hated myself, and hated my life. That night, I ate and drank my way to acceptance—or so I thought.

Father, I am such a failure. The divorce proves that. I couldn't even keep my spouse happy or married to me. I had never failed at anything before, and I didn't know how to deal with all the emotions that filled me. I was hurt, angry, disgusted, brokenhearted, and in pain. I was alone and feeling abandoned. I found comfort in food. I ate out more, sometimes with friends but mostly alone.

When I was with friends, I made healthier choices because that is what they expected. Alone, I told myself I was expanding my food palate, but I knew that was a lie. I ate no matter how I felt—sad, angry, hurt, or happy.

At each place I ate, I told myself, "This is the last time I'll eat here. Tomorrow I will start eating healthily." It was a great plan, but I never stuck with it. I continued to secretly eat my way through the pain, grief, hurt, and loneliness.

My friends and family invited me to dinners, evidently hoping that getting me back into a social setting would help me see that there was much more to life than being alone. I appreciated their efforts and found that if I played along, they would invite me out more and more. They thought I was finally on the mend, but in reality, I wanted a justifiable reason to eat. This became my new pattern—show them small signs of improvement so I could eat in peace—though that peace didn't last long.

I shopped online for clothes so I didn't have to deal with a dressing room. I refused to look in a mirror. I didn't want to see the face of failure and a body of gluttony. I taped over my mirrors at home, except for where my face showed. If I didn't see my body, I wouldn't have to accept the truth I'd see, right?

This worked well until I went on vacation and asked a friend to house-sit for me. Obviously, the taped mirror was a good indicator of the current state of my life. When she found the dusty exercise equipment and unopened exercise videos, it didn't take her long to figure out my lies and deceit.

I came home a week later to find my family and friends waiting for me, intent on staging an intervention. They were upset and started yelling at me. They took the tape off the mirrors and forced me to look. I was aghast at the sight. I didn't even recognize the person staring back at me. I was looking at a complete stranger. I saw the look of disappointment in my loved ones' eyes and felt like a failure all over again. That night, I cried for hours. The tears were hot and burned my face as they fell. Tears kept coming as my emotions raged on throughout the night. I let out gut-wrenching sobs and finally gave in to the pain of those emotions. I curled up on the floor in a fetal position and wished I had never been born. Who could love or be proud of me like this?

After that, instead of asking me out to dinner, my friends and family asked me to join them for exercise classes and workout sessions. I think I really surprised them when I said yes. I was even more surprised when I realized I enjoyed them. My loved ones began to worry less. I anticipated the times I could work out and gave it 100 percent effort every time. My instructors and fellow classmates always provided words of encouragement and told me how proud they were of my progress.

I had craved hearing those praises for so long that it gave me an excuse to go out afterward and celebrate. That led to a new pattern of self-sabotage. I worked hard at the gym, only to ruin that effort with my meals. It started as one meal on one day a week. Then it was two … which led to three, until I was "celebrating" every day. My celebration meals were a burger and fries or pizza and soda. The next day, I'd feel guilty. That guilt became disgust and shame. I so desperately wanted to change, but my worrying about it led to stress-eating. I wasn't even hungry, but still I ate. And so, the cycle of poor food choices and failure began again.

I eat when I am happy, sad, stressed, in pain, and when I am overcome with emotion. I tell myself to make better choices, but I find myself going to my favorite foods instead. I still work out because that is what everyone expects of me. I didn't put the tape back on my mirrors, but I still don't recognize the person staring back at me. All I see in the mirror are eyes full of defeat.

Every day I am tempted by food, and every day I give in. Why can't I change? Why do I always make the wrong food choices? Why can't I love myself? Why can't I break my self-sabotaging pattern? I love food and need it to survive, but it's destroying my life. Why can't I find something to love and need more than food? I want freedom from the hold that food has on me.

Zachary

When I finished reading the letter, I immediately prayed, "Father, I lift up Zachary in prayer. He is fighting a battle that is difficult to win. Father, I pray you give him strength every day and especially during the times he struggles to find a way out of his addiction. I pray for someone with understanding and patience to be a part of his life, someone who will reflect your love for him."

I placed Zachary's letter in the basket and picked up the last envelope. I noticed a flower drawn on the bottom front corner of the envelope and a butterfly on the back. The letter was on a piece of pale-green stationary, with more flowers bordering the top edge.

You are my last hope. Please help me!

I love my wife, but I just can't stop looking online at other women. It has gotten so bad that I am seeking attention outside of my marriage at work, in social settings, even internet personals. I can't find the willpower to stop.

Susie used to be so happy and full of life. Now she doesn't want to do anything. She never smiles or laughs. What is wrong with her? When I ask what is wrong, she says, "Nothing."

I was so proud to be seen with her when she took care of herself. Why doesn't she do that anymore? Doesn't she love me enough to be her best for me? What about my needs?

I have always provided her with the best of everything: clothes, jewelry, cars. I bought those things to make her happy. All I got was a forced smile and a polite thank-you. If she's not interested in showing affection, why shouldn't I seek attention elsewhere? Why can't she be what I need her to be so I can stop?

Feeling helpless!

Adam

As I finished Adam's letter, I closed my eyes in irritation. *What Susie* doesn't *need is a whiny, all-about-him husband,* I thought. Glancing down at the letter, I stopped rocking so furiously and sighed. I opened my prayer journal and wrote:

Dear Father,

Helpless? Aren't we all? Forgive my irritation, Father. Adam is in a very difficult place right now, and I pray you provide him with clarity on his situation. I pray he sees Susie for who she is and not who she used to be. Help Adam remember why he fell in love with her in the first place; remind him why you chose her to be his spouse. Help him to see that there are times when women struggle to find their places within a relationship. Our true beauty on the inside is often overshadowed by not feeling beautiful on the outside. Father, I pray that Adam withstands the temptation, but if he can't, please give Susie the strength she will need to make a tough decision on whether to stay or to leave.

Wiletta

While I walked along the shore of the ocean that evening, I thought of the kinship I felt with the letters I'd read. I have known loneliness, addiction, low self-worth, and feeling so sorry for myself that I ignored those around me. Did I so quickly turn to my Father for help? Had I trusted him for answers? Did the letter-writers? I walked back to the beach house, praying for them. I stopped as I neared the house and sat in the sand, looking out to the water. I took time to breathe and gather my thoughts. I sat in awe of the beauty surrounding me, and I offered my own prayer to my Father.

Chapter 2
SEEKING FAITH

"Go and find them."

I opened my eyes and reached to turn off a radio that wasn't there.

"Go and find them."

Sitting up in bed after a restless sleep, I realized the words I'd heard were from within me. They answered what I'd been praying since I'd finished the letters: "What's next?"

I was so moved by my experience at the beach house that I had to tell someone what happened. I knew exactly who to call—my best friend, Faith.

"Hello, Wiletta. Was he there?"

"Yes … and in ways you can't possibly imagine. I wanted to see if you would help me with something."

"Sure. What do you need?"

"I need to find some people."

"Are you in trouble?"

"No, Faith. I just need help finding the people who wrote

these letters. Since you are a private investigator, I thought you could help me."

"What letters? What people? I need to know more."

"I found some letters at a garage sale on the way to the beach house. I need to find the people who wrote them. I know I am being vague, but I really need to do this. Once you find these people, I need to speak with them."

"Wiletta, you know this is crazy, right?"

"Please, just trust me."

"Is this journey for them or for you?"

"Possibly both, Faith."

"If he met you there, then I know this journey is important, but—"

"Please, Faith. I don't yet understand why this is so important, but I feel an overwhelming need to do it. Say yes, and come with me."

There was silence on the other end of the call. I knew Faith was weighing all the options, including our friendship and her schedule, so I held my breath and waited for her answer.

Finally, she said yes.

"Oh, thank you, Faith! Do you have a pencil? I'll give you the names, so you can start searching for them. I'm leaving for home this afternoon."

Before leaving, I again wrote in my journal:

Father,

I am overcome with such myriad emotions after reading those letters. I feel like I know these people so well, simply from the words penned on each page. I feel their pain, joy, shame, and struggles to understand their circumstances. As a vessel of your love, compassion, and grace, I pray you bless my journey as I deliver my responses and that the recipients have open minds to receive them. I hope these answers provide them peace, hope, and perhaps even resolution. Father, I want to thank you for reaching me with these letters at a time when I questioned my purpose and struggled to understand my own circumstances. I pray that, together, we can help others to know your love and to help heal their hearts so they can seek you again.

With love and reverence,

Wiletta

Chapter 3
THE JOURNEY BEGINS

"I can't believe you got all this accomplished in two weeks, Faith! I believe we're ready to go!"

We were sitting in my kitchen over breakfast. The basket of letters sat on the table between us.

Faith smiled. "We're ready to go because you made some phone calls."

"We're ready to go because you did all the work! The research couldn't have been easy. Thank you, Faith. This means a lot to me."

Faith shrugged. "Finish your tea, and let's go!"

As we loaded the car and got ready to embark on our journey, I placed a hand on Faith's arm. "I mean it, Faith. Thank you. I'm glad you agreed to go with me on this journey."

"You're welcome," Faith replied. "I look forward to meeting all the letter-writers and discovering why our Father has us on this journey."

Faith sat in the driver's seat and started the car. "First stop— Joseph. Tell me; how was his mom over the phone?"

"She was cautious at first, but when I explained about the letter, she became curious about it. She told me Joseph is an amazing young man and wants us to meet him."

As we drove, I recalled Joseph's letter. The words on the page spoke of such loneliness and despair, such strong emotions for someone so young. The situation seemed impossible, and Joseph had chosen to do the only thing he knew to do—pray.

I know prayers don't fall on deaf ears. His letter reminded me of Psalm 5:3:

> In the morning, Lord, you hear my voice; in the morning I lay my requests before you and wait expectantly.

Two hours later, Faith pulled into a driveway. She stopped at the gate that blocked the entrance to what looked like—at least to me—a tropical paradise. Joseph and his mom certainly didn't live in an apartment anymore. As we waited at the gate to be buzzed through, I looked at the palm trees lining the long driveway that led to the house, which resembled a Spanish villa. The lawn and landscaping were so well-maintained, and the flowers so vivid and bright. I rolled down the window to take in the fragrant scent filling the air. The view evoked a sense of peace and tranquility.

As we walked to the door, I said to Faith, "This place feels so … I really can't think of a word to describe it."

She turned to me and smiled. "I believe the word is *alive*. Do you feel his presence here?"

"I do. Faith. I've had this feeling before but never this strong. I can't wait to hear Joseph's story."

I rang the doorbell, and a tall, thin, blonde woman opened the door right away.

"You must be Wiletta," she said. "I'm Irene. It's nice to meet you."

"Oh, it's so nice to meet you as well!" I gestured to my left and added, "This is my friend Faith."

Irene nodded to her. "Hi, Faith. Please, come in." She led us to a sitting room and invited us to make ourselves comfortable. Joseph, she told us, was finishing his chess practice session.

As we sat down, I noticed a dog lying on the floor, basking in the sunlight coming through the windows. "What is the dog's name?" I asked.

"That is Oded." Irene chuckled. "Such a strange name for a dog. I never understood why Joseph chose that name. When I asked him, he said the name was chosen by his Father. I was confused, since his father died when he was two, but I just thought it was a child's active imagination."

I wanted to tell her that I didn't find the name strange at all, but before I could say a word, the door opened, and a young man walked into the room. He had such a presence about him—powerful and peaceful—that everything, including time, seemed to stop. I instantly felt at peace in his presence. Joseph was no longer the sad and lonely young boy but was a confident young man. It had been a long time since I had encountered someone with such a strong connection to our Father.

Joseph smiled at us as he walked to Oded. He bent toward the dog, rubbed his ears, and said, "Father says hello and thank you." The dog stared at Joseph for a minute, rose to his feet, reached eye level with Joseph, and licked him on the cheek. Joseph chuckled, hugged the dog, and then patted him on the head before sitting by his mother.

"Hello, I'm Joseph. My mom said you wanted to talk about my letter. Many years ago, I hid it in a book at the library. Is that where you found it?"

"Hi, Joseph. I'm Wiletta. I found your letter with some others at a garage sale. I have no idea how they ended up there, but I was instantly drawn to them. Faith and I are traveling to meet with the writers about the content of their letters. As I read yours, I felt your loneliness. I sensed your frustration in being too young to help your mother. I also remember you asking for a friend. Did he send someone?"

Joseph smiled and said, "Yes, he sent me Oded, my dearest friend."

As soon as his name was mentioned, Oded walked over and sniffed my hand. I petted his head as Joseph continued.

"I remember the day Mom said we could get a dog; I was so excited. We went to the dog shelter, and I walked up and down the aisles, looking at each of the dogs. They were all so cute, but I was drawn to a cage at the very back of the shelter. I couldn't explain it at the time, but I knew the dog I needed was there. The night before we went to the shelter, I had prayed for help in choosing my dog. In the quietness of my room, I heard a whisper say that Oded was there, waiting for me. When I got to his cage, I bent down and whispered, "Oded, is that you?" He came to the front of the cage and licked my face, so we brought him home. When I looked up the meaning of his name—'to restore'—I knew then that our Father was going to take care of us. I call him O for short. This Oded just had his third birthday."

I raised my eyebrows in confusion. "*This* Oded?"

"This is actually Oded the Second. The original O lived a long, wonderful dog's life before he died."

At this point, Irene offered us glasses of lemonade, and we accepted, so she headed to the kitchen.

"Every day I thank our Father for O," Joseph said. It's strange, but I think Oded understands what I am saying. *Dog* spelled backwards is *God*, so maybe it isn't so strange after all. Do you find it strange, Wiletta?"

Irene walked in, carrying a tray with glasses of lemonade. "I hope you like lemonade," she said, offering each of us a glass and napkin.

"Thank you, Irene," I replied. "This looks refreshing."

"Irene, this is delicious!" Faith exclaimed.

I set my glass on the end table and turned to Joseph. "To answer your question, I don't find it strange that you made a connection between Oded and God's listening to and understanding you. Jeremiah 29:12 says, 'Then you will call on me and come and pray to me, and I will listen to you.'"

Irene, who had been sitting silently by Joseph, now said, "I agree with that passage. I do believe he listens; it is the only explanation for what happened that day."

"The day you got Oded?"

"No. This was a few nights before we adopted Oded. In fact, it has everything to do with how we got Oded. Would you like to hear the story?"

"Of course," I replied. *I think that's why we're here*, I thought.

"During that time," Irene began, "I was waitressing and had been doing housekeeping for several clients on my days off. Even with both jobs, I struggled to make ends meet. I always made sure Joseph had food and clothes, but honestly, there wasn't much left after that. That year was tough on both of us. The holidays were approaching, and I wasn't sure how I was going to get Joseph any gifts. I knew that what Joseph wanted most was my time, but without working both jobs, I couldn't pay our bills. Each night after Joseph went to bed, I cried over what I wanted to give him, compared to what I could afford to give him. I shared my thoughts, dreams, and fears with our Father. The night before everything changed for us, I told him I'd grown so weary and that I felt guilty that Joseph was spending the best part of his life alone."

Irene sighed and sipped her lemonade. Setting it on the end table, she reached out and took Joseph's hand. "I voiced my concern about the lonely life I was giving Joseph. I was worried that he would get into trouble. I couldn't buy a simple Christmas gift. I was tired." Irene smiled ruefully. "I was more than a mess. I sat on my bed and sobbed into my pillow for what seemed like hours. Finally, I became exhausted enough to sleep. As I closed my eyes, a verse ran through my mind."

"Which verse?" Faith asked softly.

"Isaiah 41:13—'For I am the Lord your God who takes hold of your right hand and says to you, Do not fear; I will help you.'"

I looked at Faith, and we both smiled because we knew our Father had probably shown up in a big way for Irene. "Did he help you?" I asked.

Irene looked at Joseph with eyes filled with love.

"Tell them, Mom," he said. "I never tire of hearing this part of the story."

Irene looked to us and said, "Do you ever wake up and feel like the weight of your burdens and worries has been lifted?"

"Yes," Faith and I responded in unison.

Irene nodded. "That morning I awoke and felt at peace. It was the strangest feeling because my circumstances were the same, yet they didn't seem so overwhelming. I was eating breakfast with Joseph before I left for my housekeeping job when—" Irene stopped abruptly but then asked, "Do you have children?"

"No," I replied for both Faith and me. "We haven't had that blessing."

"Yet," Faith added.

"I tried so hard to keep all my worries to myself," Irene said, "but children are very observant and knowing—that's especially true for Joseph. Still, he took me by surprise when he told me not to worry because I was all he needed. Joseph also told me he was going to spend his evenings at the new community center in town he'd heard about. He would participate in some classes until I got home from work. Joseph had become so withdrawn that I never expected him to want to leave the house. When I asked him what made him want to do this, he told me he awoke that morning with a verse in his mind."

We looked at Joseph, and he giggled. "You want to know the verse, right?" We nodded, and Joseph said, "'For I know the plans I have for you,' declares the LORD, 'plans to prosper you and not to harm you, plans to give you hope and a future.' That's Jeremiah 29:11."

"Did you have any idea what that future might hold?" I asked him.

Joseph nervously rubbed his hands on his pants and said, "I didn't, Wiletta, but somehow I knew everything would be okay. I didn't tell Mom that I received a letter from the center, informing me that I'd won the drawing at school for a free one-year membership. All she needed to know was that I was safe and getting involved with other kids."

"After I recovered from the initial shock," Irene said, "I kissed Joseph and thanked him for easing my worry. I didn't know about the drawing, but it makes sense with how the rest of my day went."

"What do you mean?"

"After we finished breakfast, I went to the private residence where I did housekeeping. The Millers—a young working couple with two children—would leave a to-do list on the kitchen table. On that particular day, there was a note at the bottom of the list that said I should finish quickly so I could spend time with my family, which you're supposed to do at Christmastime. I couldn't have agreed with them more! They had put only two things on their list—the morning dishes and laundry. They'd already loaded the dishwasher, so all I had to do was turn it on. When I went to the laundry room, where I found a card in the laundry basket. The card stated they'd already done the laundry, so I could leave early. They also expressed their appreciation for all I did and how delighted they were to have me as their employee."

Irene wiped at the tears falling on her cheeks and I knew the next words were going to be where our Father showed up. "They asked that I please accept their holiday bonus as a small token of their gratitude. They also told me to enjoy Christmas with my son and that they would see me in a few weeks. They gave me two weeks off and enclosed six hundred dollars—one hundred dollars for each month I'd worked for them."

"Wow!" Wiletta exclaimed. "Had they done anything like that for you previously?"

"Never anything so generous. Mr. and Mrs. Miller would leave me thank-you notes, and their children often left me pictures they'd drawn at school. The Millers are a very loving family, and they extended that love to me. I stood there a few minutes, trying to compose myself, and that's when I remembered the scripture from the night before. 'Do not fear; I will help you.' He did. And I offered him thanks."

Faith shook her head in wonder, and I said to Irene, "I'm going to guess that wasn't the only amazing event of your day, was it?"

She and Joseph both chuckled. "Oh no, he wasn't done with me yet!" Irene said. "I sat in my car for a few minutes, just taking in the sheer wonder of the events I'd just experienced. Who does that for an employee? When I was composed enough to drive, I headed to Von Tovio Diner, where I waitressed. I knew with the holidays approaching, they would be busy, and I could pick up some extra hours."

Oded, who'd been napping under the window, suddenly got

up and sat in front of Irene and Joseph. The dog whined and put his paw on Joseph's leg.

"Hey, Oded, you decide to wake up?" Joseph asked, scratching behind Oded's ears.

Irene turned to Joseph. "I meant to tell you earlier. When I was in the kitchen, I noticed Oded's water bowl was empty."

Joseph stood up. "Let's go, boy. Keep going, Mom," Joseph called over his shoulder as he walked to the kitchen, with Oded following on his heels.

Irene smiled. "Where was I?"

"At the restaurant," I prompted.

"That's right. When I arrived, I noticed many of my regular customers were there, including Destiny. As one of my more frequent patrons, we often chatted, and I knew she was traveling to see her parents for Christmas. When I took her order and inquired about her plans, Destiny told me she was leaving earlier than she'd planned because her mom was very sick. I told Destiny I would pray for them. She thanked me for my prayers and for always being the bright spot in her days when she stopped in. Destiny told me I reminded her of her mother and that helped to bring comfort in her loneliness. I thanked her for her kind words and offered her a piece of her favorite coffee cake, as my treat, for the trip. As I handed her the carry-out box, Destiny hugged me and said she would see me after Christmas. 'Safe travels, and I hope your mom's well soon,' I told her as she left the restaurant.

"As I was cleaning her table, I found a note addressed to me. I put it in my pocket to read on my break. Later, when my tables were empty, I sat at a corner booth with a cup of tea, and I read the note. As I did, tears streamed down my face." Irene reached into her pocket and pulled out the carefully folded note. "Let me read it to you," she said.

Dear Irene,

I overheard your conversation last week with your coworker about your son. I apologize for eavesdropping, but your words struck me deeply. Many years ago, I was like your son. I was very lonely and withdrawn because my mom also worked a lot. One day, she took me to the animal shelter. Mom knew if she couldn't be there that at least I would have a pet to love and keep me company.

That day I found a cat; I named her Smokey. She was a beautiful, majestic cat that became my best friend and confidant for many years to come. I'll never forget the relief in my mom's eyes when she saw how happy I was. Smokey was the greatest gift my mom could have given me. I want you to be able to offer the same gift to your son. There is enough money here to cover the adoption fee and the basics a pet will need. I'm sure, like me, your son will find a best friend at the shelter.

Destiny

Irene looked out at the sunshine. She leaned over and petted Oded, who had returned with Joseph. "And that's how we came to have this grand old master of the house."

Joseph chuckled. "And he is that, isn't he, Mom?"

Irene nodded. She turned to me and said, "I knew without a doubt this was our Father's work. I thanked him for his help and for putting the Millers and Destiny—all of these people—in my life."

"Irene that is a magnificent display of our Father's handiwork! It definitely explains the verse that came to mind when I was praying over Joseph's letter."

"Which verse was it for you, Wiletta?" Irene asked.

"It was Matthew 7:7–8. 'Ask and it will be given to you; seek and you will find; knock and the door will be opened to you. For everyone who asks receives; the one who seeks finds; and to the one who knocks, the door will be opened.' Both of you asked for his help in different ways, and he provided for you both."

"I agree, Wiletta," Irene said, "but what would you say if I told you there was still more to the story?"

Faith and I exchanged a glance, and Faith responded, "We would not be surprised, for our Father knows what we need and always provides in some manner. We know you got Oded, but what did you do with the Christmas-bonus money?"

"I was on my way to the mall when I saw a hobby store. I stopped to see what they had inside. There were numerous items from my childhood, which brought back many fond memories. In that moment, I wanted to find something for Joseph that might elicit similar feelings. I walked through all the aisles, but to my disappointment, I found nothing that I thought suited Joseph in the same way. As I was about to leave, an item on the top shelf caught my eye—a gold and silver chess set. There was a tiny trophy in the corner of the board and initials and a date beneath that. I asked the gentleman behind the counter to see the chess set. He smiled and told me it was a rare find, as not many were made from such pure metals. I gazed at the pieces as I held them and marveled at their detail and beauty. I knew there was no way I would be able to afford this, but I desperately wanted to get the set for Joseph.

"The man must have sensed my hesitation. He told me this particular set wasn't for sale. It was his, and he used as a display. He offered to show me other sets he had on sale. He asked if the set was for an experienced player or a beginner. When I told him it was for a beginner, he said he knew exactly what I needed.

"He showed me a beautiful wooden set and told me a carrying case and instruction book was included. It was on sale at under one hundred dollars. The set wasn't as beautiful as his, but it was what I could afford—especially now, with my bonus money. As I walked through the door with my gift-wrapped purchase, I heard a young man behind the counter say, 'Dad, that wasn't the set on sale! Do you want me to get her?'

"I paused at the door, ready to turn around, when I heard, 'No, son, it's okay. Someday, when you are older, you will understand why that set really was on sale.'" Irene scratched her head thoughtfully. "I still don't understand why I chose to buy a chess set for Joseph. It was the last thing I would have thought of. I didn't even know anyone who played chess."

Joseph surprised us all when he said, "I understand why."

Our ears—even O's—perked up as Irene asked, "What do you mean, Joseph?"

Joseph had such a serious look on his face as he said, "I know the man who sold it to you."

Faith and I were surprised, but it seemed Irene was even more shocked. "You do?" she said. "Who was he?"

Joseph took a deep breath and took Irene's hand. "Mom, there is something that I never told you about the Community Center."

Irene looked worried and whispered, "What is it, Joseph? Did something bad happen to you there?"

"Quite the opposite, Mom. Something wonderful happened to me there. I met a man who loved to play chess. One day, I saw him sitting alone with a beautiful silver and gold chess set on the table before him. I asked him if he knew a lot about chess. He told me that in his day, he was known as King of the Table. His name was Maximillian. I called him Mr. Max. I told him that I had received a chess set for Christmas and was trying to teach myself the game. I asked him to teach me, and we met every evening after school. He got the chess lessons approved for the after-school program, even if I was the only one interested. I would rush home from school, grab my chess box, leash Oded, and get to the center as fast as I could.

"Mr. Max took his set home, and we used mine. Each night, Mr. Max would tell me stories of his glory days and how he loved chess. Each night, I listened to his stories and his teachings on the logistics of every chess move. I fell in love with the game. He told me I was a natural.

"I'll never forget—one night before Christmas, he was running late, which was unusual because Mr. Max was always very prompt. When I asked him about it, he told me there had been an urgent matter at his store. He apologized, looked at me with a smile, and handed me a gift-wrapped box. 'Now you have everything you need to become a champion,' he said. 'Don't open this until Christmas morning.' To be honest, I was so curious, I almost opened it that night." Joseph chuckled and smiled at Irene. "You know the rest of this, Mom."

"Go on," Irene encouraged.

"When I opened the gift from Mr. Max on Christmas, I couldn't believe my eyes. When the paper was gone, and my gift was revealed, it was my teacher's grand-champion chess set—the silver and gold one that was on the table when I met him. His initials were carved next to the trophy in the corner. I knew it was the one he'd won in a grand-champion–level tournament."

Irene gasped. "What? It was the same one I saw in the hobby store?"

Joseph beamed. "Yes, Mom. The same one. Mr. Max owns that hobby shop. When I brought my set to the Community Center, he recognized it, but didn't say anything."

Irene shook her head. "I need a few minutes to take this in. Who needs more lemonade?"

"Yes, please!" we all said in unison.

With fresh lemonade in our glasses and O in his spot in front of the sofa, we turned expectantly to Joseph.

Joseph smiled. "After that Christmas, I took the new chess set to the center every day so Mr. Max could teach me using his set. I could tell it meant the world to him. He told me about meeting you, Mom, and helping you find my first chess set. I thanked him for helping you to give me the second greatest gift of my life—chess. After I won my first championship match, I tried to give his grand-champion set back to him. The silver and gold embossments were real, and it was so expensive! But he said I should keep it until I won one of my own—which I eventually did! And, well, that's where we are today. Between giving chess lessons, both online and in person, a weekly article I write for newspapers, and the monetary awards for the matches I play, I'm able to take care of my mom."

"And so much more," Irene interjected. "I was able to quit both jobs and indulge myself in gardens and flowers and landscaping. That's what I've always loved to do."

I sat there with my mouth practically touching the floor. It took me a few moments to find the words. "Wait a minute. The store owner was your chess teacher, *and* he was a former grand champion?"

"Yes, one and the same. Mr. Max was one of the greatest chess players of his time, and he passed his knowledge on to me. I picked up the game of chess quickly, worked my way through the rankings, and after a few years, I had become the best in the game. I will never forget what he did for me. He came to every match and sometimes brought his son, who eventually became my best friend. That was a time in my life when I needed a father figure, and our Father provided him in Maximillian, my chess teacher. He filled that void, giving me three people I didn't want to let down—Mom, Mr. Max, and our Father."

Faith and I sat in silence, trying to assimilate the details of their story.

Faith was the first to speak. "Our Father was weaving this story together long before you ever met Mr. Max."

"Why do you say that?" Joseph asked.

"Because of your names and their meanings. They are so fascinating and point to the Father."

Irene and Joseph seemed puzzled. "What do our names mean?" Irene asked.

"Well, *Maximillian* is Latin for 'one who is the best of the best,' which definitely applies to your teacher. *Destiny*, the lady from the diner, is Latin for 'one's fate.' Your name, *Joseph*, is a combination of Greek and Hebrew for 'he will add.' *Irene*, your name is Greek, meaning 'peace.' And we can't forget *Oded*. O's name is Hebrew, meaning 'to restore.' To put this in context, we put our fate in the hands of the Creator, who is the best of the best. He will add peace and restoration to our lives."

After a few moments of reflecting on Faith's explanation, Irene said, "It seems we were all destined to find each other—to become one big happy family."

Joseph looked at his mom. "We definitely were, Mom. We started as nobodies, but as it states in Romans 9:25, 'I will call them "my people" who are not my people; and I will call her "my loved one" who is not my loved one.' That is how I feel—like I was nobody, and our Father sent me Mr. Max. Mr. Max became a father figure to me and helped me to learn a game that, ten years down the road, helped me to take care of you and allow you to spend more time with me. I am eternally grateful for everyone he put in my life and in my path to help me become the man I am today."

Chapter 4
KATERINA

The following weekend, Faith and I were once again on the road. From the driver's seat, Faith glanced at me as I adjusted my seat for the fourth time.

"You didn't sleep well, Wiletta?" Faith asked.

"I never have a good night's sleep in a hotel. The bed was okay, but it wasn't my bed. Next time, let's try to find a bed-and-breakfast."

Faith nodded. "Sounds good to me. You have time to take a nap. We won't be there for a couple of hours."

"That's okay. I can't sleep in a car either."

"I keep thinking of Joseph. His was such a heartwarming story. I'm always amazed by the work our Father does in our lives."

"I know, Faith, but sometimes that can be so difficult to remember."

"Did you ever get in contact with Katerina?"

"No. I left a few messages, but she never called back. I'm nervous about this. How will she react to two strangers showing up on her doorstep? Maybe we should have waited."

"I'm sure it will be fine, Wiletta. Remember who's in charge of this journey! Besides, my work schedule is crazy the next couple weeks. This was the best time for me for a two-day trip."

"Katerina's letter was so full of pain and sadness," I mused aloud. "I hope our showing up with her letter doesn't cause her more grief."

"Yes, but you said you have something to share with her. More than the letter?"

I smiled. "A promise of joy."

As we pulled up to the house, we grinned at each other, took a deep breath, and exited the car. We walked up the driveway, lost in our own thoughts. As we reached the door, together we prayed, "Father, please open everyone's minds and hearts to hear your words. In your holy name, amen."

Before we could even knock, the door opened, and a young man, skateboard in hand, almost walked into us. He stopped abruptly, surprised to see us. "Who are you?"

I stepped back, finding the courage to speak. "Hi. I'm Wiletta, and this is Faith. We're looking for Katerina."

"She's not here."

"Is there a better time to come back?"

"No." The young man looked down and sighed. "She's dead." He looked at me curiously. "You're the lady who left the messages. What do you want with my mom?"

I was still processing the news of her death when it hit me that he said he was her son. "Excuse me—did you say you're her son?"

"Yes. My name is Hans. Katerina was my mother."

I grabbed Faith's hand. "May we come in? We have something

of your mother's that we would like to share with you. I think you will find it very interesting."

"You have something of my mom's? Come in. Wait here. Let me get my dad."

We stepped inside and closed the door. As Hans went in search of his father, I asked Faith, "Did you know she passed away?"

"Yes. I found her obituary in my research. She died of cancer. Maybe I should have told you, but I didn't want you to change your mind about coming." Faith smiled. "I looked up their names, Wiletta."

"Katerina Simeon." I nodded. "And?"

But before she could reply, Hans and his father walked toward us.

Hans's father seemed to hesitate but then continued toward us and held out his hand. "I'm Amon. Katerina was my wife." His face was a mixture of surprise and what looked like hope, which struck me as odd, given we were strangers who had appeared on his doorstep. If I hadn't known better, I would have said Mr. Simeon was expecting us.

"Hello, Mr. Simeon," I said, taking his hand. "I'm Wiletta, and this is Faith. We're sorry for your loss."

"Thank you. Hans tells me you've left several phone messages, which he deleted without telling me." He glanced at his son.

"Sorry about that," Hans murmured.

"Hans also says you have something of Katerina's. May I see it?"

"Certainly, Mr. Simeon. Is there somewhere we can sit and talk?"

Amon said, "Please. Come this way."

We followed Amon into a sitting room with one of the most exquisite garden views I had ever seen. Mr. Simeon paused at the window, wiped a tear from his cheek, and appeared to be quietly praying. I was awestruck by the sight of the pink dogwood tree in the center of the garden. The tree was in full bloom, and its petals lovingly lay on the grass surrounding the tree. I noticed Mr. Simeon was not focused on the tree but on the wooden bench to the right of that tree. The back of the bench formed two hands, one across the other, as if they were holding something. Above the hands was a heart. The bench itself was gorgeous, but my eyes were drawn to the blue lotus flowers surrounding the bench. The flowers were blooming just outside of where the dogwood petals stopped falling. I made a mental note to ask why those particular ones were chosen.

"Beautiful, isn't it?" Hans said. "It was my mom's favorite place."

"I can understand why she loved it there; it's a stunning sight—so exquisite, vibrant, and peaceful."

Mr. Simeon looked at me when I said *peaceful*. He smiled and made his way to a settee with two chairs on either side. As soon as we sat down, Faith opened her iPad and started typing.

As we sat down, I got the strangest feeling that Amon knew exactly why we were there and what we had come to discuss. Suddenly, I was nervous as what we were doing dawned on me— two strangers coming into someone's home with a letter that might evoke complicated feelings. I was so distracted in my worry that Amon had to repeat himself.

"Wiletta? You found it, didn't you?"

"Found what?"

"The letter."

"Amon, how could you possibly know about the letter? Or that I found it?"

"It's the only reason that makes sense for why you would come to see her. And it's the answer to my prayer."

"Dad, what letter and what prayer?"

"Son, during a dark time in your mother's life and our marriage, I encouraged your mother to write a letter to our Father. And I pray every night for your heart to heal from your mother's death."

"Grandfather never said anything about a letter."

Amon smiled. "Son, it wasn't written to your grandfather, but a Father of a different nature."

"I don't understand. If it wasn't grandfather, then who was it?"

Faith and I sat quietly, knowing we were witnessing someone seeing our Father's power for the first time.

Amon turned to Faith and me. "Before I get to that, I need all of you to understand that Katerina was a wonderful and loving person. She gave so much of herself to others. Those characteristics drew me to her. When we met, I rarely spent time doing anything other than work. She showed me how much life I was missing by not spending time with others, especially with her. She taught me that we were created to live in community with others."

Amon paused to follow the motion of a butterfly that flew into the garden before he continued. "Two years later, we were married. Life was good, and we were happy, but Katerina had times of extreme sadness. The sadness would diminish her light, and when I asked why she was sad, all she would say was that she felt incomplete. I struggled to understand because, for me, Katerina was all I needed in life; she was my gift from God. But Katerina desperately wanted to be a mother. I never understood her obsessive need for a child, but I said I would do anything to make her happy, so we tried to get pregnant."

He sighed, and I touched his shoulder lightly. "Were you successful?" I asked.

"Yes, after a few tries, and Katerina was happier than I had seen her in months. Her happiness filled me with such joy! And every day I thanked God." Amon wiped his eyes and sighed. "But twelve weeks later, Katerina miscarried. We both grieved for the baby that we lost. And we worked through our grief in different ways. I lost myself in work, starting earlier and staying later. Katerina's grief turned into depression. I didn't know what to do to help her, and so I did the worst thing and stayed away. There were times I felt as though I was losing her. I prayed for God's help, and he must have heard me because Katrina would come out of her depression and engage in life again. Things were good again for us and between us. Some months later, Katerina got pregnant again. And again, Katerina was full of hope and joy. I loved seeing her like that. She had such a glow."

Amon suddenly stood and walked to the sliding glass doors that opened to the garden. "But once again, Katerina miscarried." He turned to us and said ruefully, "We started to slip into the same pattern as before—Katerina's depression and me working too much." Amon returned to sit next to Hans on the settee.

"Gosh, Dad," Hans said, taking his father's hand.

Amon squeezed his son's hand. "We're getting to the best part, Hans. This time, Katerina found a volunteer position at the orphanage. Working at the orphanage brought Katerina's light back. Every day she would come home and talk about the children and how she loved being there. Every day I thanked God for providing healing and for the happiness returning to our home. Each month I'd send an anonymous donation to the orphanage.

"A year later, Katerina called me at work. She was ecstatic, and I knew something monumental had happened. She gleefully told me she was pregnant. I was surprised and delighted. We hadn't talked about trying again. We'd simply been finding joy in life and in each other. But my delight quickly turned to fear. I didn't want history to repeat itself. I wasn't sure either of us could make it through that again.

"I'm sure Katerina was anxious also, but the closest we came to talking about it was when we decided to wait until after the fourth-month ultrasound to furnish the baby's room. Then we'd know blue or pink, although Katrina teased and said a light green was good with her. 'As long as the baby is healthy,' she'd said. Each week was agonizing. We wanted to feel joy, but instead, we were overwhelmed with worry. Week twelve came and went. I was so happy to pass that awful milestone. I was still apprehensive, though, and still praying for our baby's survival.

"The week after our you're-having-a-girl ultrasound, Katerina called. She rarely called me at work, so I knew what she was going to say. We had lost this baby too. I was devastated. I scaled back my hours at work to spend time with Katerina, so we could grieve together. What we couldn't do together was pray. How could God give us this hope and again take away that gift?" He shook his head. "I am so sorry. I don't know where my manners are. Would you like something to drink? I can offer ice water, tea, coffee, and I think Hans has a few bottles of Gatorade."

"Ice water would be wonderful. Thank you," I replied. "Faith?"

"Ice water is fine."

Amon stood. "Hans, come with me. You can put cookies on a plate while I pour the drinks."

After they left the room, I said quietly, "Oh, Faith, the heartbreak!"

Faith nodded in agreement. "And withdrawing from God when they needed him the most."

Amon and Hans returned with ice water and cookies. "We're a bachelor house, so I hope you weren't expecting homemade cookies!" Amon settled again onto the settee and continued his story. "One day at work, I was having lunch with a colleague, John, and sharing with him what had happened. I told him Katerina and I were more supportive of each other than we had been with the previous two miscarriages, but we'd stopped going to church. He listened intently, and when I was finished, he said quietly, 'We rarely understand our Father's plan for us. Or his timing. But we are assured that even if we don't know, he knows and wants what is best for us.'

"I asked him, 'Do you really believe that?' He smiled and said, 'I do. My wife and I experienced a similar situation as you and Katerina. We never understood why God wouldn't bless us with a child. Eventually, we came to accept his decision. Years later, we were given tremendous joy and fulfillment, leading the children's missions at our church. His plan did not include a child of our own, as we wanted. Instead, we were given the opportunity to help and love thousands of children. We will always be thankful to our Father for his decision.'

"I never knew that about John. His words had such an impact on me! I thought maybe God's plan for us was simply different from what we wanted. Eventually, I started praying again, asking not only for healing but also for him to show us his plan for Katerina and me."

"Did he?" asked Hans, reaching for another cookie.

"Yes, Hans, he did. Why don't you pass those cookies around the room, son?"

Sheepishly, Hans leaned toward me, handing me the plate.

"My stomach dropped when Katerina called me at work a few months later. All I could think was, 'Father, not again!' But I was relieved to hear her tell me the orphanage had a full-time position available. She asked what I thought about her applying for the job. I told her I thought it was a great idea. John's words came to mind, and I hoped this was God's answer to my prayers.

"Katerina got the position, and the change within her was immediate. She was her true self again—loving and hopeful, but more important, full of joy and purpose. I loved listening to her tell me about the children and how they simply needed a little bit of inspiration and a lot of love. I told Katrina often that her heart was big enough to shower them all with the love they needed. She'd smile, and I knew God had provided a way to heal her heart. He'd given her a way to be a mother, even if the children weren't ours naturally. To so many children, she was the only mother they knew.

"Months later, Katerina got very sick. We thought she had the flu. It broke her heart to stay away from the orphanage, but she couldn't go to work when she was sick. On the fourth day, I told her, 'Let's get you to a doctor and find out what's going on.' Katerina didn't like doctors, but she eventually agreed. I took off work, and we went together to her appointment—only to be shocked to hear that Katerina was pregnant."

Amon shook his head. "You're supposed to be excited to find out you're going to be a parent. But we were overwhelmed with shock, fear, and apprehension. Though she couldn't say the words, her eyes betrayed her feelings. Katerina was as afraid as I was. Could she survive another miscarriage? Survive emotionally, mentally, spiritually? All I could do was hold her and try to reassure her. With eyes full of love, I told her, 'Even if this isn't in his plan for us, somehow, some way, we will make it through this together, as we have always done. You are his gift to me, and I refuse to let you go!'"

"Wait, Dad," Hans interrupted. "You mean I was going to have older sister or brother? I don't mind being an only child, but that would have been awesome!"

I saw the sadness enter Amon's eyes, and I knew we were only now coming to the most painful part of Katerina's story. I reached out to place my hand on Hans when Amon said, "Yes, Hans." Amon cleared his throat. "Please be patient, son. I'm reliving emotions I put away years ago. I'm trying to keep them at bay, so you will know your mother's story."

I gave Hans's hand a squeeze as Amon started speaking again.

"Every night I begged, cried out, and pleaded with God to let us have this one. As the weeks went by and the baby stayed alive, we allowed ourselves to feel hope. When weeks turned to months without complications, we allowed ourselves to feel joy and prayed hope would stay in our lives. We started to plan for the baby's arrival. We bought pregnancy books, looked at baby furniture catalogs, and picked out colors for the baby's room. When we learned we were having a girl, we were overwhelmed with joy and excitement. We named her Angelique."

I said softly, "Like an angel."

Amon smiled. "Yes, that was her name because to us, she would be our very own angel." He took a few deep breaths before he continued. "We prepared her room—pink, of course. We sang to her. And read to her. And prayed over her. Each day we were full of awe, wonder, and joy that we'd created a life to be brought into this world. I always thought Katerina had a special glow about her, but this was different. Reminded me of the halo of an angel. I know that sounds strange, but—"

"No, it doesn't," Faith interrupted. "Not at all."

"I never wanted to see that glow leave her, but—" Amon's voice broke and tears ran down his cheeks. "But at eight months, Katerina got an infection, and our Angelique died in the womb. Our little angel was stillborn. We were so devastated."

Amon had to pause. We were all crying, feeling his sorrow. Faith handed me some tissues from her purse. Hans ran from the room and came back with a box of tissues. He grabbed a handful and handed them to his dad, then grabbed some more for himself.

"Katerina sobbed uncontrollably. I cried out to God, 'Why now? Why let us get this far only to rip our child out of our reach?' Then we started second-guessing and blaming ourselves. We must have done something wrong for this to have happened—again. But the doctors advised us that the condition was rare and had nothing to do with what we did or didn't do. Katerina and I looked at each other and our eyes told the same story—how would we ever survive without our little angel?"

Faith and I watched Hans and Amon hug each other so tightly that I wondered how they could breathe. This was a pain so deep and raw that only God, the Father, could heal it. I was anxious to hear this part of the story, but we all needed a few moments to allow our hearts to grieve the loss of their children—especially Hans, who'd never known how many siblings he'd lost.

After a few moments passed, Amon patted Hans on his back and held him at arm's length to look at him. "You okay, Hans?"

Hans nodded.

Amon walked to the window to gaze at the garden. When he spoke again, we could hear the pain and agony in his voice. I asked if he wanted to stop, but he said, "No, I need to finish … to tell you the rest of Katerina's story."

Amon turned back and looked to Hans. "When we came home from the hospital to an empty house, we were sad—and angry. The pain was overwhelming. But more significant, we had lost faith. For that, I am terribly ashamed, but I couldn't get past the loss of Angelique. And I lost Katerina too. She took a leave of absence from the orphanage and withdrew from everything and everyone. She refused to leave the house and spent most of her time grieving in Angelique's room. She would allow me to hold her and cry with her, but when I tried to talk with her, she'd push me away. I watched her slip farther away from me and our life together. I was worried we wouldn't survive all the loss and heartache. I knew if we were going to survive, it was a burden that I alone would carry.

"Remember John? The colleague I spoke of earlier?" Amon looked to each of us as we nodded. "When he returned from a year-long overseas mission trip and heard our news, he came to see me. I'd missed our conversations and was glad to see him. I knew when he walked into the room that he could help. There are times when you just know our Father sends someone into your life to help save you. I had pulled so far away from God. I couldn't see beyond my pain to understand that I needed him more than ever. But our Father never left me, not even when I cried out in so much bitterness and anger.

"John hugged me and said, 'There are no words that I can say to convey how sorry I am for your loss. How are you doing?' I remember being angry at the question. How was I doing? How did he think I was doing? But all I could do was shake my head and tell him how terrible the hurt was and that I couldn't pray. John held me and said, 'Losing your daughter is a tragedy. Allow yourself time to grieve and fully feel every emotion. I'll walk with you on this path of healing, brother.'

"Then John asked me to go to his house for dinner that night. I didn't want to leave Katerina, but I couldn't say no. Something inside me yearned to be with John and to believe what he was saying to me. When I got to John's house later, I was disappointed to see I wasn't the only one in attendance. There were at least ten other men sitting in his living room, eating off paper plates on their laps. When John saw me standing at the door, he smiled and said, 'Father says hello. Welcome to my Bible study group.' I wanted so badly to leave, but that yearning returned, so I sat down and listened. That Bible study had such an impact on me and helped me understand how to help Katerina.

"We spoke of many people in the Bible, but none resonated with me more than David. Father took his child too but later blessed David in many ways. Despite his pain, David's faith in our Father never wavered. I knew that I needed to find my faith, so I kept going to the Bible study each week. But even as I was finding my faith again, Katerina withdrew even farther. Every night I prayed for healing for both of us and for a way to help her.

"One night during my prayers, an idea popped into my head—I would have her write a letter to our Father. In this letter, she could express all her feelings, while still reaching out to him. When I suggested this to her, Katerina was uninterested. When I told her I thought this could be an answer to my prayers for her, she relented and sat down at the table to write her letter. She asked me if I wanted to read it. I told her I didn't need to and that I was proud of her for writing to our Father. Then I took her hands and prayed that our Father would answer her. I never knew what happened to the letter. I just assumed she threw it away.

"Shortly afterward, I bought this house and began building this garden for Katerina. My hope was that the beauty of the garden would draw her out of the house. Katerina had always loved flowers. I planted the dogwood to remind us that our Father had lost his child too. Legend says the dogwood's petals have an indentation on them to signify the area where the nail was used on Jesus's cross. When they bloom in the spring, I am reminded that out of deep agony and tragedy something beautiful can emerge."

"Beauty from ashes," I heard Faith say softly.

Amon smiled. "Exactly. I picked pink petals for Angelique. The garden is a reminder that our Father gave us eight joyous, beautiful months with our precious daughter, and that she will forever be in our hearts. I built the bench to signify that only together can our hearts heal and become whole again. I wrote this all in a letter I gave Katrina on the anniversary of losing Angelique.

"As the tree began to grow, Katerina began to spend more time in the garden, especially in springtime. It was as if she needed to be there when the first petal fell. I will never forget the sight of coming home to find her in the garden, cradling the fallen petals with a look of awe and wonder on her face. She heard me approach and turned to me with a smile and tears streaming down her face. She thanked me for the garden. I thanked God, knowing Katerina was healing."

We all jumped when a drum riff suddenly filled the air.

"Sorry," Hans said sheepishly. "That's my phone. Can I answer it, Dad? It's Elaine."

"Sure, son, go ahead. We'll wait."

As Hans talked on the phone, Faith, Amon, and I walked to the glass door to admire the garden.

"We spent a lot of evenings together in the garden," Amon said. "The beauty and peace we felt sitting on the bench together gave us the strength to grieve—together—for our little girl. We became stronger as a couple and in our faith."

Hans returned and, seeing his father's questioning eyes, said, "We're going to the mall later for a movie and pizza."

Amon nodded, then turned to Faith and me to continue his story. "Katerina went back to work at the orphanage. Being with children every day helped her heal. She often spoke fondly of one particular little boy. He was around five years old and had lost both his parents in a tragic traffic accident. Katerina said he was quiet and sad and didn't play with the other children. He and Katrina were drawn to each other, and she spent extra time with him. When she spoke of him, I saw a look of love in her eyes that I thought was lost forever. God had provided a way for Katerina to be a mother after all. I planted the blue lotus flowers in the garden to symbolize what was previously unattainable—the day we brought our son, Hans, home."

I saw the look of astonishment on Hans's face. "The lotus was for me?"

"*Hans*, meaning 'gift' or 'blessing,'" Faith interrupted. "*Amon*, meaning 'man of faith.' *Katerina*, meaning 'pure.' *John*, meaning 'God is gracious.'" Faith saw us staring at her and said, "I'm sorry I interrupted. I love names and their meanings."

"Yes, Hans, the lotus reminds us of the blessing—the gift that you were and still are—to us from God."

"That's why she loved the garden so much, Dad. It healed her and reminded her how much God, our Father, loved her."

"Yes, son. And to remind her that *she* was my blessing, an

otherwise unattainable gift from him. Now, I hope it will bring you healing too."

"The last words she said to me, Dad, were to go to the garden, and I would find healing there because I'd always find her there."

Amon pulled Hans into a big hug. "Yes, Hans, and you always will."

"Amon," I said, "would you like to read Katerina's letter? The notes on the last page are what I felt spoke to me while I prayed over her letter."

Amon nodded, and I handed him the letter. He held it as if it was a fragile piece of glass. He took a few minutes to run his hands along the envelope and then he took a deep breath and opened the envelope. As he pulled the letter out, he asked, "How did you come across the letter?"

I watched as he gently opened the letter and ran his fingers across Katerina's writing. "I acquired it and a few others at a garage sale."

Amon looked up in surprise. "A garage sale?"

"Yes. As I read each letter, I prayed for an answer, and I wrote what I felt our Father was conveying through his words to me. When I read Katerina's letter, I felt not only the pain but also the overwhelming anger for the loss of her children. I prayed for words of healing, and I felt the Father showing me resolute love and an abundance of hope."

"Please tell me what he laid on your heart about my mom's letter," Hans said. "I need to know."

"Sure, Hans, as long as your father is okay with it."

"Dad?"

Amon looked up from reading the letter. He looked back and forth between Hans and me, and slowly, he began to smile. "Go ahead, Wiletta."

Turning to Hans, I said, "Our Father spoke of her body being weak and that childbirth would kill her. He couldn't let that happen because her gifts and purpose in life had yet to be fulfilled. He took her first three children because they wouldn't survive childbirth. He gave her eight months with Angelique to feel the joy and love she could offer a child. He wanted her to know that you don't need a blood tie to be a mother, and she would do wonderful things as a mother to many. He spoke of numerous children who had never known joy or hope but only fear and pain. The children would find not only hope but love through Katerina. And she would see their love for her when she looked into their eyes. He wanted her to remember she was a true daughter of Christ, and he loved her even in her anger, when she didn't love him."

"Your mother's heart had an endless capacity to love," Amon added. "The children reminded her of her worth. There were times she'd come home and almost shout 'I am so blessed! By the children, by you, by my beautiful garden!' In one of our healing moments in the garden, our Father reminded us that he knew the devastating grief of losing a child. His only Son and light to his world was nailed to a tree to die. His Son suffered such agony, while our Father suffered the overwhelming pain of having his child taken from him. He was very angry but still heard his Son pray for forgiveness for those who hurt him. He granted Christ's prayer. And after the cross, he welcomed his Son home, just as he welcomed our children—a place surrounded by love, where no one feels pain."

"Isaiah 40:10–11," I said softly. "'See, the Sovereign Lord comes with power, and he rules with a mighty arm. See, his reward is with him, and his recompense accompanies him. He tends his flock like a shepherd: He gathers the lambs in his arms and carries them close to his heart; he gently leads those that have young.'"

Amon wiped a tear from his cheek. "God longs to mend shattered hearts."

"She needed to take time to grieve, to feel her anger, yet remember that he would never leave her," Faith said. "There's another passage in Isaiah 40:28–31. It says, 'Do you not know? Have you not heard? The Lord is the everlasting God, the Creator of the ends of the earth. He will not grow tired or weary, and his understanding no one can fathom. He gives strength to the weary and increases the power of the weak. Even youths grow tired and weary, and young men stumble and fall; but those who hope in the Lord will renew their strength. They will soar on wings like eagles; they will run and not grow weary, they will walk and not be faint.'"

"Hans, our Father never left your mother," I told him. "He stayed with her until she was ready to seek him again. He heard her prayers, in addition to all those from others on her behalf."

"He certainly heard mine, Wiletta. Every night I prayed she would become my mother. When she took her leave of absence, I sometimes prayed two or three times a day, asking him to bring her back, and he did! The happiest day of my life was when she and Amon came to tell me that they were adopting me. I didn't know our Father then, but I definitely knew he heard my prayers."

Amon and Faith were wiping tears from their cheeks. Amon leaned in and murmured something in Faith's ear, which brought a smile to her face. She said something in response, and I made a mental note to ask her about that.

I turned to Hans and smiled. "It wasn't a coincidence that you and Katerina found each other."

"What do you mean?" he asked.

"Remember what Faith said your name means? Hans is Scandinavian for 'God is gracious.' Your last, Simeon, in French, means 'God has heard.' So, you see, Hans, you truly were an answer to their prayers. You were born to be their unattainable gift."

Hans shook his head with emotion. Unable to speak aloud, he hugged me and whispered "Thank you, Wiletta. I do believe you are right. I was meant to be theirs. I miss my mom terribly, but now I know that not only her presence but also that of our Father is with me every day. I'm going to spend a lot of time in the garden, like my mom did. And I'll ask him to help mend my heart."

We spent more time with Amon and Hans, talking about work and school and skateboarding. Our Father's presence was so strong that we were reluctant to leave. Amon and Hans walked us to the door, and as we walked away, I heard their next words.

"Son, would you like to sit in the garden with me?" Amon asked.

"Yes, Dad. I'd like that."

Faith and I made our way to the car. When we got inside, I asked her, "What did Amon say to you when I was talking to Hans?"

"He asked me if I knew whether PI stood for *private investigator* or *personally invested* with regard to me and my work."

"What did you tell him?"

"I told him it was probably a little bit of both, but I was sure our Father would say *personally invested*."

Chapter 5
CRISTINA

"Thank goodness it stopped raining," I said as I opened the car door. Fastening my seatbelt, I glanced at Faith. "Do you want me to drive? Are you tired?"

"No, Willetta. I'm good. I'm saying a quick prayer for the trip and Cristina."

"We should probably stop somewhere for a quick lunch before we get to her house. I'd hate for my stomach to rumble in the middle of a conversation."

Faith giggled. "Sounds like a great idea. We don't need that interruption!"

Several hours later, I continued the conversation I'd begun at lunch. "Each letter spoke to me differently. When I read Cristina's letter, I thought about my dad. He's always there for me. I can't imagine not having him around."

"And our Father is always is present. Sometimes his help comes to us differently than what we want or feel we need. I'm sure our Father helped Cristina." Faith stopped and parked the car. "Now that we're here, let's find out how his grace changed her life!"

As we walked to her house, I prayed for Cristina and that I would find words of comfort for her.

Faith knocked on the door.

"Who is it?" asked a voice from the other side of the door.

"Wiletta and Faith. I called a few days ago concerning a letter. We're looking for Cristina."

The door opened abruptly. A tall woman stood there, looking incredulous. "*The* letter?"

"The one you wrote to our Father."

"Yes, that one." She shook her head. "I guess I didn't believe when you told me over the phone that you'd found it. I wrote that during one of the toughest seasons in my life."

"May we come in?"

"Oh my, please forgive my lack of manners. I'm Cristina, and yes, please, come in. I was just making hot chocolate. Would like to join me?"

Faith answered. "We would love a cup, Cristina."

Cristina led us to the living room. "I'll be right back. Make yourself comfortable, please."

As she went to make the hot chocolate, I looked at Faith. "She seems happy, doesn't she?"

Faith nodded in agreement. "I have a feeling her story ended exactly where our Father intended."

Just as I was going to ask her to elaborate, Cristina came back. She set the mugs down and took a seat on her sofa. She looked to both Faith and me, took a deep breath, and said, "I am really surprised you found that letter, especially since it, along with a photo of me and my dad, was hidden in the wall of my bedroom in my childhood home. I never expected to be talking to someone about that time in my life, but honestly, I am glad you found it. Would you like hear why I wrote it?"

"Certainly—as much as you're comfortable with sharing," I replied.

Cristina seemed relaxed, agitated, and excited all at the same time. "To understand the letter, you need to know about me. You see, my dad was larger than life. He was my original superhero, and I thought he would always be there for me. I was too young to understand the temptations of the world, so when he said he was leaving, I instantly thought it was something I did. My mom assured me many times that wasn't true but that they just couldn't be together anymore. On some level, I knew my mom was right, but what does a ten-year-old kid really know of the world anyway?

"My dad left, and Mom worked hard to provide for me. I missed my dad all the time. But I thought missing my dad was doing a disservice to my mom. I was sad and feeling guilty. I buried those feelings very deep and stopped trusting everyone. People would make promises throughout my life, but I never expected them to deliver. And many of them didn't. However, much to my surprise, two people did in a *big* way."

"Who were those two people?"

Cristina leaned over to pick up a throw pillow at the end of the sofa. "My mom made this. Isn't it pretty?" Hugging the pillow tightly, she said, "I want you to know that I made some very bad decisions in my life, and I have suffered the consequences of those decisions. Many of those decisions included relationships with men. I wasn't wise enough to understand that I always looked for someone to fill the void my dad left. Of course, other men could never do that, but that surely didn't stop me from trying. I went to many parties, looking for love and putting myself in dangerous situations.

"One night I left a party with a group of friends; we all had been drinking too much. We were in an automobile accident, and I was injured very badly. I don't remember much about the ride to the hospital because I kept losing consciousness, but I do remember the EMTs telling me to find something to cling to because my life was precious, and I needed to fight for it. I didn't have the energy to respond, but I remember hearing a male voice say, 'This is not the life I had planned for you.' At the time, I had no idea who the voice was, but my response to the EMTs' instruction was to think of my mom. They found her number in my purse and called her.

"Mom dropped everything to come to me. I still remember when she arrived. The look on her face would have stopped my heart, had it not been hooked to a monitor. She was absolutely devastated. She tried to maintain a calm façade, but I could see the fear and pain in her eyes. She held my hand as they wheeled me to surgery. When they said she had to let go, she leaned over to kiss me and said, 'I didn't abandon you then, and I certainly won't do it now. I will stay here as long as it takes for you to come home, my daughter.' Right before they put me under for surgery for my broken ribs, shattered leg, and fractured skull, I heard the same male voice I'd heard in the ambulance repeat my mom's words. I thought I was losing my mind.

"The surgeries were successful, but the road to recovery was very difficult and painful. True to her word, Mom stayed by my side in the hospital and took me home with her to recover. Over the many months of rehabilitation, she took care of me. Each night she would come in and read the Bible to me and pray for my healing, both physically and mentally. I never told her that sometimes I only pretended to be asleep because I was afraid she would leave the room if she knew I was awake. I appreciated everything she did for me, and slowly I learned how to trust again; my mom was definitely worthy of that trust.

"Once I had recovered enough to resume a 'normal' life, my mom said she wanted to talk to me. I had dreaded this conversation because I didn't want a lecture. I was certain she was going to talk about the men and the partying and her disappointment in me, but she didn't. She talked about my childhood. She told me I was old enough now to understand the circumstances of my dad leaving and that she had blamed herself all these years for my wild ways. Mom told me that I needed to understand that there was no option for her and Dad to stay together because their words and actions toward each other were so harmful. She also said that now she realized she should have looked for someone to be a father figure in my life—she believed that would have changed the trajectory of my life. She told me that she prayed daily for me to realize the men I was spending party time with could not give me the unconditional paternal love I was seeking.

"Mom whispered that she had finally found a man who could

be that father figure I still needed and who would love me more than I could imagine. I thought she was going to tell me she was getting remarried, but Mom looked at me and said she wanted me to hear what he wanted to say to me. Then she handed me something I thought I would never see again—my childhood Bible. She'd given it to me after my dad left. Each night, we'd read together and pray."

Cristina sighed. "My mom took care of me in the best way she knew—with love in her heart and our Father's words in her hands. She said *this* was the man she'd found for me. As I took the Bible from her, Mom told me to remember that *this* man never left me. 'He watched over your youth, and he protected you in the crash,' she said. 'Now he wants you to know him again.'"

It was clear that Cristina needed a few minutes to compose herself, and honestly, I did too. The first part of her story broke my heart, but when she spoke of her mother, my heart burst with joy. Her mom came in her time of need and brought with her the man she knew Cristina needed—our Father! Faith handed us both tissues. As we voiced our thanks, she turned to Cristina and said, "Clearly, one of the people who kept promises was your mom. I am curious what she promised you."

Cristina stood up and picked up picture on her mantel. Handing it to Faith, she smiled. "This is my mom. She made three promises. The first was to always love me, regardless of the things I said or did. The second was to always provide for me the best she could. And the third was to be there to rescue me when I needed rescue. After the accident and subsequent recovery period,

I realized she had already upheld the first and second parts of the promise."

"And the third part?" I asked.

"The third part she fulfilled the moment she handed me that Bible. She may not have known it then, but she rescued me from the dangerous path my life was on. Mothers know best, right?"

"Yes, they certainly do," Faith agreed. "Was our Father the second person?"

"Yes, he was. I went back to church and started making new friends and strengthening my relationship with our Father. He helped me find answers to some of the questions in my letter. He taught me that not everyone is meant to stay in my life forever, and when they leave, it is not because of me but because their season is over. It says in Ecclesiastes 3:1, 'There is a time for everything, and a season for every activity under the heavens.'

"I admit learning to have people in my life for only a season was a hard lesson to learn but one of the most valuable. He also taught me that before I could truly love anyone else, I had to learn to love myself. And the key to healing is letting go. I had to let go of the emotions tied to my dad's leaving."

"Three promises, three lessons," I mused out loud.

"That's right!" Cristina returned to the sofa. "Perhaps one of the best things I learned was that people leaving doesn't mean I have some kind of defect that chased them away. The more time I spent with our Father and the people in my church, the more I understood that the people who are meant to stay will stay, and those who aren't, won't. These same people became the stable figures in my life that had always seemed to elude me. It turns out

I needed the right people to stay in my life for the right reasons. I remember lying in bed one night, and as I drifted off to sleep, I heard that male voice again. He said, 'Welcome home, daughter.' That was the best night's sleep I'd had in a long time. I finally found the love I'd always searched for."

I looked at Faith and could tell we were both affected by Cristina's tale. "Cristina, your story is so moving. I am awestruck by your narrative. As I told you on the phone, I prayed over each letter and then wrote in my prayer journal what I felt was our Father's answer. May I share that with you?"

"Oh yes, Willetta! Please!"

"The words penned in your letter were wrought with pain and despair, which compelled me to say this prayer: 'Dear Father, one of the worst feelings in the world is feeling all alone. I pray you surround Cristina with your love until the one thing she knows for sure is your presence. I pray in her time of need that she calls out to you to shine light onto her darkest times. I pray your presence in her life will give her hope for better and brighter days to come.' I feel he was present throughout your life, whether it was watching over you as a child or even, as your mom said, that he protected you in the accident. I don't feel like he ever left you. I believe that sometimes it's very difficult to feel his presence or see handiwork in our lives. We spend so much time searching for what eludes us that we miss what he is already giving us."

"I agree, Wiletta. I spent so much time putting myself in harm's way that I missed his guiding hand. I was so focused on what I didn't have and the pain from my past that it took me a long time to see the things I did have—my mom and hope for the future."

Faith asked, "Do you find it easier to see his presence in your life now that you have a closer relationship with him?"

"Looking back, I can see his existence, especially after I got my life straightened out and moved closer to my mom so we could continue rebuilding our relationship. One day, as we were talking, I mentioned to my mom how much I yearned to have a relationship with my dad. I told her I was sad because I didn't think that would be possible, since he probably never thought of me after he left. I told her he probably considered me a mistake."

"That's a terrible thought. How did your mom react?"

"Mom told me that wasn't true, and she would prove it to me. She left the room, and I thought I'd really upset her. Had mentioning my dad hurt or angered my mom? I got up to go find her just as she came back into the room. She had a package wrapped in Christmas paper. I was very confused. I asked her how this proved her point. She told me to stop talking and open the gift. I tore the wrapping paper, excited to see what was inside. I opened the box and was left speechless. On top of a scrapbook was a picture of my dad, holding me as a baby. I looked at my mom with tear-filled eyes. Mom told me it was time I knew how much my dad truly cared for me, that I should look in the scrapbook for proof that he never thought I was a mistake. In fact, he considered me a gift he didn't deserve.

"I remember gently lifting the photo frame from the box and lovingly tracing my dad's face in the photo. After a few minutes, I set the picture aside and pulled the scrapbook from the box.

'Daddy's Little Girl' was stamped on the front of the book, and inside were photos of him at all my school events, pictures of me, and newspaper and magazine clippings of articles about my accomplishments. I asked Mom why he'd included pictures of himself. She told me the pictures were included so I would know that he was there. It turns out that even though he wasn't visibly active in my life, he didn't miss anything I participated in.

"There was a postcard at the bottom of the box. I turned it over and read the note on the back. The message said, 'When you are ready, I'll be waiting for you,' and it had my dad's address. I felt a seed of hope begin to grow. I looked longingly at my mom. She told me it had been a few years, but he was still there waiting for me. I didn't think it was possible to cry any more tears, but they continued to pour from my eyes. I picked up the photo again and whispered, 'Is it possible?' I hugged my mom tightly and thanked her for this incredible gift."

"Why do you think she kept the box from you for those few years?"

"Timing. Dad asked Mom to wait until she thought we were both ready. Mom told me after he left the military, he had a lot of problems. They gave him pills for his depression and pain, and, well, the pill taking got out of control. He's a recovering addict. That's why they got divorced and why he stayed away. He had to get clean and sober. And then my life got a little crazy. Mom knew I had a lot of healing to do—emotionally facing the consequences of my actions, getting over my love/hate feelings for Dad." Cristina chuckled ruefully. "A *lot* of healing. For both of us. Mom wanted me to have a relationship with my dad. She knew if

I saw him stoned, depressed, or manic, it'd be emotional overload for me. And if I started spiraling out of control that would make being clean and sober difficult for him. I'm glad she waited."

"Cristina," Faith said curiously, "you don't have to answer if you don't want to, but did you go see your dad?"

Cristina smiled and said, "I did. A few days later, I found my dad waiting for me on his front porch, just as the postcard said he would. At first it was awkward because neither of us knew what to say. Then he told me of the love and joy he felt when he'd held me as a baby and that he knew our Father had given him a gift he didn't deserve. We shared stories and laughed and enjoyed catching up with each other. Over time, the bitterness left my heart and was replaced with joy. I finally had both my parents in my life, and that was a wonderful feeling."

Cristina's smile wavered. She stood up and paced around the room, murmuring to herself. "I'm okay ... I'm okay."

I stood up to intercept her. "Cristina?"

Cristina stopped and turned. Stepping to me, she took my hand. "Really, Willetta, I'm okay." She returned to the sofa, picked up the pillow, and hugged it to her chest. She sat down with a sigh. "One year later, to the day, I received a call that my dad had died of a heart attack. I was devastated! I'd just gotten him back, and now he was gone again, but this time he was gone forever. I didn't think my heart could handle the agonizing grief of his loss.

"Three days after his funeral, I received a letter in the mail from my dad. I almost didn't open the letter because I thought someone was playing a cruel joke on me. But when I did open it, the letter really was from him. Dad expressed his regret over not being in my life and that he wished he would have chosen differently. He spoke of his happiness when I was born and his fear that he could never be a good dad to me. He reminded me that I was a gift from our Father above. Dad wrote that he didn't want to tarnish my life with how he responded to tragic memories that haunted him. He told me of the nightmares he experienced, stemming from his time in the military, and that he struggled to control his emotions. Sometimes he cried, sometimes he was in a rage, and sometimes he was like a zombie. He'd thought he made the right decision by leaving, but instead, he realized he should have gotten help. Then he could have been there as I grew up.

"Thinking he would never see me again, my dad expressed how happy he felt when I walked onto his porch. That he cherished all our talks. He ended the letter by saying he would miss me, but when I was ready to come home, he would be waiting for me in heaven. I believe his last act on this earth was to heal the wound left by his abandonment. He wanted me to know his decision to leave was *his* decision and that I was *not* the reason he left. Even in his last moments on earth, he was thinking of me."

"Cristina, I am at a loss for words right now," I said. "It appears your dad knew he was going to die and wanted to help you to make peace with your childhood. Faith, what do you think?"

"I think it took a lot for your mom to give you that present, and it shows just how much she loves you. Your dad wanted you to be happy, and he knew the only way to do that was to provide healing for your childhood wounds. Even in his final days, he wanted you to know how deeply you were loved—and would still be loved, even when he was gone."

Cristina took a few moments to let our statements sink in. She took a deep breath and wiped the tears from her cheeks. "You are both right. I know our Father knew exactly what I needed—a mom who rescued me, even when I didn't know I needed to be rescued. He also gave me a man who I didn't know as a daughter but as a friend, one who was there to listen and offer words of encouragement when times became tough. I'm grateful for both of them and for our Father bringing them both back into my life."

"Would you say you are finally at peace with your childhood trauma and with your dad?"

"I am. I believe when the world became too much for my dad, our Father took him home to give him comfort. We both were seeking peace, and our Father granted that serenity to each of us in different ways. When I feel saddened by my dad's loss, I am comforted by the verse in 1 Kings 8:57—'May the Lord our God be with us as he was with our ancestors; may he never leave us nor forsake us.'"

"Why that verse, Cristina?"

"He was with my dad in life and in death. He was with my mom. He healed all of us. And I'm grateful our Father never left me, even when I left him. He showed me that not everyone had left in my life."

Before we left, I asked Cristina if her mom knew about his final letter.

"She hadn't known," Cristina said, "but she was not surprised he wrote it. During that call, I thanked her for giving me that unopened Christmas gift. I thanked my mom for truly being there for me. I told her how overjoyed and relieved I was that she was okay with my reconciliation with my father. I heard my mother's unconditional love when she said, 'Cristina, I would walk to the ends of the earth and sacrifice everything to bring you happiness.'"

"Your mother is quite remarkable," I told her.

"I agree," Cristina said. "She also is a gift from God."

We said our goodbyes, and as Faith and I walked to the car, we spoke of Cristina's story and that our Father did amazing works within her life.

"Before we walked into Cristina's home," I told Faith, "I was searching for words to comfort her. But she didn't need comfort from me. In fact, I think I was the one who needed the reassurance of our Father's presence. Her story is a comfort to me."

Chapter 6
ZACHARY

"Do you see it?"

Faith and I drove slowly down a residential street, looking at house numbers. The car's GPS had announced our arrival at a vacant lot, so we turned it off and looked for the house the old-fashioned way.

"Got it!" Faith exclaimed. "There on the left."

As she pulled into the driveway, Faith asked, "How did the conversation go with Zachary's niece?"

"Valentina is still grieving Zachary's passing from four years ago. I hope we can bring her some peace. She's curious about the letter."

"We're early, Wiletta; let's sit for a minute." Faith unfastened her seat belt and turned to me. "This one hits close to home for you, doesn't it, Wiletta?"

"Oh, Faith, Zachary's letter was heart-wrenching. His struggle with food was so sad. The addiction consumed his life, and he was unable to escape its grip. I'm not sure if I'll be able to keep it together and stay focused on Zachary and Valentina."

"I know this visit will be very difficult for you, Wiletta, but our Father would not ask this of you if he didn't think you could handle the situation. Think of it this way: your background with addiction makes you the best person to speak with Valentina. Because you've been through this yourself, you understand Zachary's battle and his choices."

"What did I ever do to deserve a friend like you? You believe in me, even when I don't believe in myself."

"You asked our Father for help, and he sent me to you. Zachary did the same, and we were sent to Valentina." She nodded toward the house. "It's time. She's watching us through the window."

We got out of the car and started walking toward Valentina's house. But I had to stop. I was so nervous that I felt a panic attack coming on.

Faith rubbed my arm. "Breathe, Wiletta."

I took a few deep breaths. I was feeling more anxious than nervous. I kept wondering how my own battle with addiction would affect the conversation. And how would Valentina react, knowing I survived my addiction but her uncle didn't? I recognized the old familiar feeling of survivor's guilt rising within me.

Faith saw it too. "Stop it. Your story has its own purpose. It may help her, or it may not, but either way, the fact remains that you survived to tell the story. You may have to tell it today, and if so, then you will tell it with thankfulness and gratitude to our Father for saving you. Everyone's story, while often difficult to relive, is meant for a greater purpose. Never lose sight of that!"

I knew Faith was right. Our stories aren't about us but how our Father saved us and uses our stories to help others. If Valentina needed to hear how I overcame the power of addiction to heal, then I would tell her.

Before we could even knock on the door, Valentina opened it and said, "Wiletta? Faith? Please come in."

We followed her inside and were led to her kitchen. My eyes were drawn to the pictures on the wall. Valentina noticed my interest and told me, "That's my uncle Zachary."

The photos were from various years of Valentina's life. In all the photos of the two of them together, I saw a look of absolute love in Zachary's eyes as looked at his niece. Most people wouldn't think anything of this, but as a recovering addict, I know that addiction's power overshadows everything and everyone in your life. Zachary's love for Valentina transcended the addiction. I made a mental note to share this with Valentina before we left.

We sat at the kitchen table, and Valentina offered us coffee, tea, and biscotti. We sipped our drinks and ate our biscotti in silence. I suddenly wasn't sure how to start this conversation, but it was Valentina who spoke first.

"I want you to understand that my uncle was a good man. He was kind and caring and my favorite person in the world. My dad died when I was very young, and Uncle Zachary stepped in and assumed that role in my life. Anytime I needed him, he was there, even when I called him in the early morning hours. Not many people would be happy with a kid calling to cry about the boy who broke her heart or to ask for help with homework, but he always picked up the phone. He listened and offered guidance. He saved me from considerable heartache and kept me on the right path, but I was unable to save him."

Tears spilled from Valentina's eyes, and in that moment, I knew she blamed herself for his death. She didn't understand that some people cannot be saved—or don't want to be saved—from their addiction. Sometimes, not even the overwhelming love they feel for someone can overcome the addiction's damage to the body.

"Valentina," I said, "I want you to know that—"

"Please don't. Please let me finish. I may never find the courage to discuss this again. Today, I am prepared to relive these memories and feel the pain, but tomorrow may be different."

I nodded and then looked toward Faith. While Valentina and I had been talking, neither of us had noticed that Faith had gotten up and was looking at the culinary arts school certificates, awards, and photos of Cristina and famous people that lined a wall. Now, she turned to us, and her eyes gave away her thoughts. I knew she was reliving the harrowing time of helping me overcome my alcohol addiction. The raw pain in her eyes surprised me. I never knew the full extent of her pain during those times, but now, it was clear that she had suffered a great deal. I closed my eyes because I couldn't bear to see the depth of her pain, knowing that I had been the cause.

I felt a hand encircle mine and give a squeeze. I opened my eyes to see Faith sitting beside me.

"It's okay," she whispered. Faith looked at Valentina and said, "You are a chef and a teacher? I would say a very good one, based on the certificates and photos on your wall."

Valentina smiled. "Yes, I am. I'll get to that part of the story shortly. I never knew the real reason for the onset of Uncle

Zachary's food addiction, but I always assumed it had to do with his being lonely after his divorce. I tried to tell him that Aunt Jackie's leaving was the best thing for him because she treated him terribly. But what did I know? I was a kid when she left him. Uncle Zachary was so sad for years after that. He said the only bright spot in his life was me. I told him he was the most important person in my life, and he needed to stay there. He always said the same thing: 'I will be here as long as I can, and even then, I will never truly leave you.' I think, even back then, he was trying to prepare me for his loss.

"For years, family and friends watched as my uncle spiraled out of control. Every time someone tried to help, they would eventually give up and say he was a lost cause. I never thought that, and when my other family members and his friends talked about staging an intervention, I agreed to help. We weren't prepared for what we saw that day, and neither was Uncle Zachary. We are a large Italian family. Imagine his surprise when he walked in his house and saw thirty of us. To say he was shocked is an understatement.

"We went to Uncle Zachary's house that day with the intent of helping him, but I think we just made matters worse. He always accepted invitations to dinner but always passed on hosting any family functions. We never thought anything of it and just attributed it to his having a bachelor-pad lifestyle. That assumption never prepared us for what we saw when we entered his house that day. We expected there might be empty food containers everywhere, but there weren't any to be found. We did find an excess of unhealthy food in his pantry and refrigerator.

Everyone panicked and reacted by instantly devising a plan to help him overcome his issue. I left everyone in the kitchen and went to explore the rest of his house. When I looked around, I knew we were dealing with a much bigger issue. Uncle Zachary had taped over all his mirrors.

"I came out of the bathroom at the same time he entered the house. My uncle was surprised to see me. He smiled, and then the rest of the family descended on him. Everyone was talking over each other and pointing toward the kitchen. His smile slowly faded away, and in his eyes, I saw defeat; his secret was out. He sat down and got an earful from everyone. I remained in the hallway, blocking everyone's view of the bathroom. I didn't want anyone to see the mirror because I was afraid this intervention would reach a new level. When Uncle Zachary turned to look at me, I whispered, 'I love you no matter what.' He forced a smile and whispered the same to me.

"Our relatives were so busy lecturing him that they didn't see the defeat and shame I saw in the eyes. It was then that I made a huge mistake; I went to him, hoping to offer some comfort. As I knelt next to him, I heard a collective gasp—the others had seen the mirrors. Everyone rushed to the mirrors. They stared in horror at the sight of the taped mirrors and began tearing the tape off at a feverish pace. The whole time, they just kept yelling at Uncle Zachary, asking why he couldn't love himself enough to stop, telling him to think of what this would do to the family. I wanted to scream at them to shut up, but all I could do was stand by him as he flinched with each criticism. I saw the pain and defeat in his eyes; that was when I vowed to save him myself."

As I looked from Valentina to Faith, I recognized the feeling revealed in their eyes—guilt. One felt guilty because she hadn't seen the signs of addiction in her friend, and the other felt guilty because she couldn't save her uncle. I heard Valentina's words before she uttered them: "It's my fault."

I knew that telling her she was wrong wouldn't help her see the truth, so I asked her, "Why do you feel that way?"

"If I had become a chef sooner, I could have helped my uncle eat better. I could have shown him more love and appreciation. Maybe he would have fought harder. I should have stood up to my family when they criticized him. I could and should have done more so Uncle Zachary would have wanted to live more than he wanted to feed his addiction." Every word she said pierced my heart and ripped through my soul because the same words were said about me, years ago.

I struggled to rein in my own feelings. Valentina needed reassurance, but I couldn't seem to shake my own memories to find the right words. My recollection was so vivid and overwhelming that I could hardly breathe or gain control of myself. I knew Valentina was still talking, but I couldn't tell you anything she said. I knew this letter delivery would be the hardest, based on my own battle with addiction, but I never expected it to trigger me so badly.

I was ready to excuse myself when I heard Faith's gentle voice say, "You did more for him than you realize, Valentina. You saw the absolute worst side of him and still loved him. You showed him compassion and unconditional love when others didn't. You—and only you—were the reason he kept fighting his addiction. There was nothing more you could have done for him."

"How can you know that?"

"I watched my best friend struggle through addiction. I loved her through it. But I always struggled with the guilt of not being able to fix it for her. I felt so helpless at times because I couldn't save her from the addiction's grip. I told myself I failed her as a friend because I wasn't enough for her to break the addiction's hold on her."

"What happened?"

"I sought counseling, and it was the best decision of my life. My counselor told me it wasn't my job to fix her but to love her on her worst days, as much as I did on her best days. She helped me see that for her to survive, she needed to be the one to break the addiction's hold on her. I learned that she had to become stronger than the addiction, and I had to prepare myself in case she couldn't become that strong. Those were some of the worst years of my life. I spent them loving her, but sometimes I was angry that she wasn't winning the battle. Nevertheless, I stayed by her side, constantly telling her how much I needed and loved her."

"Was she able to overcome the addiction?"

"Yes."

"How did she do it?"

Faith paused and turned her tear-filled eyes to me. "You can ask her yourself. Wiletta was that friend."

Valentina looked shocked as she turned to me and said, "Really?"

I nodded in response. Then I squeezed Faith's hand and said

to her. "I never knew how my addiction affected you. I'm truly sorry for what I put you through and so thankful you stayed by my side."

Faith returned my squeeze. "I never would have left your side."

"I know. That has meant more to me than anything else." Turning to Valentina, I said, "Yes, Valentina, I am that friend."

"How did you—I mean, why did you ..."

I saw Valentina struggling to voice her thoughts, but it didn't matter because I knew what she was thinking: why did I live and her uncle die? That was a question that many people, including addicts, often wonder the most, yet they rarely find the answer.

"Valentina, please don't go down that rabbit hole," I said. "It won't give you any answers, but it will certainly add to your guilt. I don't know why I was chosen to survive, but I believe it was to help others understand addiction. Choosing alcohol over family and friends was a painful way to live. My addiction had a stranglehold on me, and the path to recovery was a long and difficult one. I did well for a few weeks, but then I would relapse. That was my pattern for a few years."

Valentina nodded. "My uncle did the same. It was always a roller-coaster ride with him. I never knew if or when he would relapse. I'm sure that's how I learned patience. I spent time with him during the relapses, always wondering why I wasn't enough for him to stop."

"One thing you need to understand is that addicts must want to quit," I told her. "They also need to have a support system in place for when the cravings return because they *will* return. But even if they found something greater than the addiction to live for, sometimes the body is just too damaged to function properly. Your uncle gave you what he could in his condition."

"I believe that. He told me during his final days that loving me was the only thing he succeeded at in his life. He said he failed every time he tried to overcome his addiction, and no one cared or tried to help him until I came into his life. He spent so much time with me so that I would have more good memories than bad ones, once he was gone. Later, when he was in the hospital, I begged him to keep fighting and told him I only had a few months left in culinary school. Then I could cook for him all the time, and together, we would beat the addiction. He smiled and told me that he would hold on as long as he could, but he was getting tired. I thought he only meant he was tired that day. As I turned to leave, he said, 'Pickle, make sure you love food for the right reasons. Use food to help others and not to hide your pain, like I did. Food is meant to be enjoyed and can bring people together.' I smiled and told him I would do just that, and I would cook him a fabulous meal on my graduation day."

Faith looked at me, as we simultaneously asked, "Did he make it to your graduation?"

Valentina closed her eyes, and tears rolled down her cheeks. She strained to find her voice. "No. He died the night of the last practical portion of my final exam."

"Were you there?"

"Yes. When I passed my last practical and knew I would graduate, I drove to the hospital to tell him the good news. I planned our celebratory dinner while driving there, and I couldn't wait to share it with him. There was no one I wanted to celebrate this achievement with more than my uncle. As soon as I walked in, Uncle Zachary asked if I passed. I nearly shouted yes! My uncle was very weak and rarely smiled, but he did then, and in that moment, it was like all the stars combined into one to light the room. He beamed with joy and pride. 'I'm so proud of you, Pickle,' he said. 'Go make your mark on the world. Show them how food can heal bodies and why people should love food.'

"I promised him I would and then said I wanted to tell him about our celebratory dinner the following night. 'I'm going to need a rain check, Pickle,' he told me. When I asked him why, he didn't answer. I asked again. He looked at me, smiled, and mouthed, 'I love you.' And then the alarms on his machines went off. The medical staff ushered me out of his room. The doctor eventually came out and told me Uncle Zachary had had a massive heart attack, and they couldn't save him."

"I'm so sorry, Valentina," I said.

"Thank you. The next day, I cooked that celebratory dinner for both of us. I celebrated my future and his freedom. Do you think he is at peace?"

"Yes, I do. I think your uncle wanted to hold on long enough to make sure your life's path was set on its rightful course. His body just couldn't properly function any longer. When I read your uncle's letter and prayed for him, I was confused by the message I received, but now it makes sense."

"I never knew he wrote the letter. What was the message?"

"It is from 1 Corinthians 10:13—'No temptation has overtaken you except what is common to mankind. And God is faithful; he will not let you be tempted beyond what you can bear. But when you are tempted, he will also provide a way out so that you can endure it.' We all have temptations, Valentina. Some people have more than others. I think you were God's answer for your uncle's addictive temptations. With you, he was able to resist and enjoy life. I think his death helped you stay on the course he wanted for you. You became a world-renowned chef, and you teach workshops about eating healthily while focusing on keeping the food flavorful. You did it for him, didn't you?"

"As difficult as it was to do, it was the only way I knew to honor him. After my celebratory dinner, I wanted to give up because cooking would always remind me of him and make me sad. At first, it was very painful, but then I remembered all the times we ate together. I felt such joy; my heart burst with love at the memories. I feel like my uncle is still with me when I cook, so I continue cooking and studying different cuisines. This way, I keep him close, and he was right—food healed my grief. I want to celebrate my uncle and honor his memory, so I created a scholarship at the local culinary school in his name."

"You've done so well, Valentina. I know your uncle would be so proud of you. Just curious—why did he call you Pickle?"

"What a strange nickname, right? I hit a rough patch in my life and my studies. I told him that I could quit and still be a good chef. He told me I could quit, or I could withstand the hard times and become a *great* chef. I asked him to explain why I would want to endure all that hardship. His response was, 'So you can become the pickle!' I looked at him like he was crazy and asked what a pickle had to do with anything. He explained that if I stopped my studies, I would be like a cucumber, or I could persist and become a pickle. Both are good enough on their own, but the pickle persevered to become something different, something more, than what it originally was. He smiled and said, 'I hope you choose to become the pickle, my dearest niece.' I chose the pickle." Valentina smiled. "I have a small pickle design I'm going to put on the aprons my staff wears, as well as on the corner of my menus, to remind everyone to be something different and original and better."

I placed my hand over my heart, touched by the sentiment. The pickle represented the last tie to her Uncle Zachary, and Valentina's pickle design was endearing.

"Valentina, not only are you an amazing chef, but you are also a compassionate person. You've survived a great tragedy with your uncle's death, yet you can celebrate his life and his memory. You looked past the addiction and saw the best in him. Not many people can do that."

"Really?"

"Yes. When I finished rehabilitation, I went to see my pastor. I told him I felt called to help others, but I wasn't sure they could see me as anything but an addict. He told me to remember what was said in 1 Samuel 16:7—'The Lord does not look at the things people look at. People look at the outward appearance, but the Lord looks at the heart.' You did the same for your uncle. You looked past his addiction to see his pure heart. That, Valentina, is the greatest gift an addict can ever receive."

"Thank you, Wiletta. I appreciate you and Faith coming to see me today. I finally feel peace about my uncle. I believe your pastor was right about using your story to reach others. I never expected to feel anything other than guilt, but your presence here has changed that. Please don't let anyone or anything stop you on this journey."

Faith and I each hugged her and said our goodbyes. As we walked to the car, Faith squeezed my hand tightly.

"How are you doing?" she asked.

"Surprisingly, I am doing well. I needed this visit as much as Valentina. Our Father showed up in a big way today. It seems he brought healing to all of us."

"Yes, he did. I believe the purpose of this particular visit can be found in Mark 5:34. It says, 'Daughter, your faith has healed you. Go in peace and be freed from your suffering.'"

Chapter 7
ADAM

Because of our conflicting work schedules, Faith and I had difficulty finding time to complete our journey. In one of our phone conversations, when trying to find a day good for both of us, Faith said, "I think the time is another gift from our Father."

"I think so too!" I agreed. "I don't know about you, but I needed this time to process everything we've heard about the need for our Father's presence, remembering he is always with us. That's what drew me to the beach house. I am healed and comforted by hearing others share how he sent healing and comfort. Does that make sense?"

"Yes. Complete sense," Faith said. "I've been thinking of the stories and all the lessons we've learned."

"By the way, when I spoke to Adam, he asked us to meet him at a coffee shop close to his home."

"Why not his house?"

"He said it would be easier for him to talk about his letter in a public yet somewhat private venue. Do you remember his letter?"

Faith nodded. "Yes. He was married to Susie but was watching online videos of other women. I wonder if his meeting in a public place has anything to do with his letter."

I thought for a moment and asked Faith, "In what way?"

"Well, being in public would limit his access to the internet and subsequently finding women like those he referenced in his letter."

The following week, I reread Adam's letter as Faith drove us to the coffee shop where we were to meet him.

Faith glanced over at me and noticed I was shaking my head. "Okay, what's wrong?"

I sighed again—as I had done as I read the letter. "I'm having a hard time not being irritated with Adam, and I haven't even met him!"

"Why?"

"Well, he starts by saying, 'I love my wife, but ...' Then he makes a lot of 'I' statements—I just can't stop, I was so proud of her, I always provided for her—and then it sounds like he blames his wife, Susie, for the problem."

"Let's wait and hear his story, okay? It sounds like a tough situation for both him and Susie. Remember who directs us on this journey."

"You're right. I know."

"I'm sure healing will happen," Faith said.

We walked into the coffee shop and found Adam waiting for us in the far corner, away from other seating, although he didn't need to sit there for privacy—he was the only customer in the shop.

"Adam?"

He seemed startled and rose to greet us. "Yes, sorry. I was lost in my thoughts. You must be Faith and Wiletta."

"We are. May we sit down?"

"Yes, please do. Thank you for meeting me here. I knew this discussion could be very difficult and emotional for me. I'm hoping that being in public will help me keep it together."

"We understand, Adam. But please know we're here to return the letter to you. You don't need to tell us why you wrote it."

"Thank you for saying that, but I want to tell you, if you have time."

I felt Faith nudge me under the table as she said, "Of course, Adam."

"I tossed that letter in the recyclables, with old phone and cable bills. I never thought anyone would find it. You can imagine my surprise when I heard from you, Wiletta. I'm not proud of that period of my life. I was forced to face a lot of issues within myself. In some ways, that letter was very cathartic, yet in other ways, it was very damaging."

"Damaging?" I said. "How so?"

"That's quite confusing and contradictory, isn't it? Let me explain. First, I want you to know that Susie was and still is a beautiful, caring, and wonderful person. She didn't deserve any of the grief and heartache I caused her. I admire her for staying as long as she did. Lord knows, if the roles were reversed, I would have left much sooner."

"Susie left you?"

"Yes. At the time, I couldn't understand why, especially since I refused to acknowledge I had a problem. Even as she was leaving, she was still determined to help me. She found a counseling center and made an appointment for me."

"Did you go?"

"Not to that particular appointment, but Susie was relentless in her efforts to help me. She kept scheduling appointments, and I kept canceling them until finally, she picked me up to 'talk.' It turns out that her idea of talking was a couple's session with that counselor."

Perplexed, I said, "Even though you were no longer a couple, she still scheduled a couple's session?"

Adam laughed. "Her unrelenting nature was one of the attributes that made me fall in love with her. But when I realized what she'd done, I didn't feel very loving toward her. I wanted to scream at her and leave, but she told me I owed her at least one session. She was right, so I stayed. That day started a journey that would span many years. By writing a letter to our Father, I was able to release a lot of bottled-up emotion, so the letter was cathartic. But I also had to face that my actions had damaged our relationship past the point of restoration." He paused and studied me for a few moments. "You're struggling to understand Susie's actions, aren't you?"

He had read me correctly. I was never good at hiding my emotions, and this time was no different. "Yes, I am. I remember the horrid words you spoke about Susie in your letter and how you justified your actions because of what you saw as her shortcomings. How could she be so dedicated to helping you after what you said and did?"

"Susie is the most considerate and giving person I know. Also,

I wasn't always that negative. She always remembered the person I *was*, even when I was awful to her." He sighed. "Susie and I met when we were young and became best friends. Eventually, we married. The early years of our marriage were the honeymoon ones; we only had eyes for each other. Then life got in the way. We found ourselves working jobs with long hours, and we spent less time together. As the months and years went by, it was harder to stay invested in our marriage. We tried, but I'm not sure either of us tried hard enough. Eventually, we both turned to other avenues to fill the void and fulfill our needs. Susie spent more time with her friends, and I spent more time online." Adam examined his coffee cup. "I could use some more coffee. Can I get you something?" he asked as he stood up.

"I'll go with you," Faith said. "Wiletta drinks tea, but I'll join you in a latte."

"Thank you, Faith."

As they walked to the counter, I said a silent prayer of repentance for judging Adam. When he and Faith returned to the table, Adam began without preamble. "I gave in to the tempting ads. And I watched videos of other women. At first, it was just their stories and their daily activities, but it soon turned into much more. I started talking to other women online about immoral topics. I began to compare Susie to those women and wanted her to be more like them. So I started dropping hints. I'd mention how someone I'd met online laughed at one of my jokes. Or how I saw a picture of an attractive woman with a hair color I liked. Or the dress she wore." Adam looked down at his hands. "I'm so ashamed. I told myself that Susie would hear them as hints to help her, to help us."

He looked up and caught Faith and me sharing a look. "You're right," he said. "Disgusting, isn't it? Of course, Susie didn't hear hints. She heard insults and how unhappy I was with her. Slowly, Susie did start to change. She became more despondent each day. She was no longer her happy and carefree self. She blamed herself for not being enough for me anymore. Susie became a shell of her former self and alienated herself from everyone. I, on the other hand, continued living my double life—good guy doing great things by day and wicked guy doing wicked things by night. We both spiraled out of control in our own ways, it seemed."

Adam had been relatively calm until this part of his story. Now, his voice seemed to catch in his throat, and he was clearly overcome by pain. "I'm sorry," he said. "Sometimes the memories bring forth more emotion than I can handle."

"It's okay," Faith said. "Do you want to stop?"

"No. I need to finish." Adam took a deep breath. "You know about the misdeed, so you should also know about the healing. I never harmed Susie physically, but we both inflicted so much damage on each other mentally. I became bitter and sarcastic. Susie's words were hurtful and accusing. We became so angry that we lashed out at one another and stayed in that pattern until the day Susie told me she was leaving. Like an idiot, I asked her why. Her response was not what I expected.

"Instead of blaming everything on me, which was completely valid, she quoted Proverbs 6:32—'But a man who commits adultery has no sense; whoever does so destroys himself.' Susie

89

told me she would not destroy herself by committing adultery out of revenge, and there was no way she could stay in our relationship because of my adultery."

"Before she said that, had you recognized your online activity as adultery?" I asked.

"No. It wasn't until Susie forced me to go to that counseling session that I understood the connection between a nonphysical internet relationship and adultery. When that happened, I realized the full extent of what I had done. I can sum it up with 1 Timothy 6:9. 'Those who want to get rich fall into temptation and a trap and into many foolish and harmful desires that plunge people into ruin and destruction.' I destroyed our relationship and ruined my name, but the worst part was that I hurt Susie so badly that I almost destroyed her too. I was so blinded by my temptation and sin that I couldn't see what my adultery was doing to our relationship—I came to realize that through the counseling sessions. The weight of my guilt and shame overwhelmed me. I didn't know how to fix what I had broken or how to make amends with Susie. I tried to make it right, but all my attempts were met with silence.

"My counselor told me this was a time to work on myself, so when Susie was ready to talk to me, she'd be able to see and hear the differences in me and not the hurt. I had to face the worst parts of myself and make difficult decisions to get my life back on track. I continued with counseling and found a support group for my addiction. Most important, I found a church. Slowly, my life started to turn around. I learned ways to redirect my temptations. I became more involved in my church and community. I found closure for much of my past and past transgressions—except for how I'd hurt Susie. No matter how much progress I made, the weight of not making things right with her weighed heavily on me."

"Making things right with Susie was important to you?" I asked.

"Oh yes!" Adam's voice became animated. "I knew how much blame Susie placed on herself. At the end of our marriage, she felt she would never be enough for anyone. I wanted her to understand that I was the issue and not her. I needed to apologize for my actions and for any pain I'd caused her. We both needed healing, so we could move on with our lives, even if it was without each other. Above all else, I needed Susie to know that she was always enough and always beautiful, inside and out, even when I was blinded by my choices and made her feel as if she weren't."

Adam looked around the coffee shop, which was getting busier with the after-work rush. "We met for coffee in this very place and spoke of our relationship, our mistakes, and our hope for our futures. I apologized for my actions and the pain I'd caused her. I told her she was not responsible for anything I did; that I'd got caught up in my sin and singlehandedly destroyed our relationship. I thanked her for dragging me to counseling because that saved my life. She wanted to know why I felt she needed to know these things. I told her I didn't want her to go through life wondering why our marriage didn't work and what she could have done differently. I wanted her to know she was worth more than I could ever offer her."

"What was her response?" Faith asked.

"She thanked me and told me that I was worth more too. We left that day with peace in our hearts and feeling the beginning of closure—that we could finally put that time behind us."

We fell into silence, thinking about Adam's story. I reached over and touched his hand gently. "After I read your letter, Adam, I prayed for healing and an answer. The verse that was laid on my heart is from 2 Corinthians 5:17, which says, 'Therefore, if anyone is in Christ, the new creation has come: The old has gone, the new is here!' Susie saved your life that day by putting you on a path to develop a relationship with our Father."

"I agree. Our Father saved me by giving Susie the courage to leave. If she'd never left me, I would have never stopped my activities or found our Father. And in his grace, I've been asked to share my story with young men and women, to tell them about the dangers of online temptations. I hope it will make them think twice before heading down the path I chose."

We were thrilled to hear that his story was meant to help others. As I handed Adam his letter, I said, "I wonder if it could be used in some way when you give your talks to others. Thank you, Adam, for sharing so openly with us."

"I feel a little more of God's presence each time I share my story."

As we reached our car, Faith said, "That was truly an amazing story of our Father's guidance to a path of redemption. More than that, though, I was struck by how much Adam and Susie truly cared for each other. After all the pain and heartache they both experienced, they met to try to bring closure to each other's wounds. In the end, it seems their friendship was strong enough to want the best for each other, even if that meant not being together."

"I agree," I said. "I was struck by how Adam's story was focused more on giving Susie peace than on his own healing. He seemed so selfish in his letter. I didn't expect him to be concerned with her well-being, but I'm glad he recognized that Susie also needed that closure to heal from the past."

Faith nodded. "Grace, healing, and transformation—our Father's story."

We headed home, each of us lost in the wonder of God's love.

Epilogue

Faith and I met at our favorite restaurant to celebrate the journey we'd taken together. She suggested we each write a letter to our Father about our experience and share them with each other.

After we asked the waitress for hot tea, Faith smiled and said, "I must admit that when you first called me, I had no idea where this trip would take us or what it might bring us. I'm glad I went because reading the letters and then meeting the writers or those left behind was an amazing experience. To see how our Father touched all their lives brought joy to my heart. Each story was filled with such emotion that, at times, I thought I would be too overwhelmed to appreciate their journey. Instead, I was comforted by our Father's presence, not only in their lives but also with us on this mission. I'm so grateful you called me that day."

"I'm so happy you agreed to go with me, Faith. I thought the journey would be difficult, and I couldn't imagine having anyone with me but you. Your faith in our Father has always been strong. I'm glad we shared this together."

The waitress approached with two pots of tea, and I thanked her. As I looked for a mint teabag, I said, "I wrote my letter. Did you write yours?"

Faith reached in her purse and pulled out a pale-yellow envelope. "Let me read mine first."

"Of course."

"Father, thank you for loving me when I felt unlovable, for being there when everyone else left, and for putting people in my life who love me as I am. Thank you for blessing me each day with a chance to help others. Thank you for Wiletta's friendship and the chance to accompany her on our adventure. I'm grateful for how you touched not only the people we met but also Wiletta on this journey. If my faith in you is as strong as Wiletta says, Father, it is because of how strongly I feel your presence in my life."

Faith folded her letter and looked at me with a raised eyebrow. "Yours?"

"Before I started writing, I thought of each person we met on this journey and how their stories showed me that our Father is never far from us, even when we can't feel his presence. I recalled that as I listened, I saw myriad emotions on their faces, but the most prominent one was peace. I realized that the journey was not meant just for them but also for me. I was meant to find what I was missing in my life—our Father. I went to the beach house to find an answer to that prayer. This journey was the answer."

Tears glistened in Faith's eyes. I opened my letter and read it to her.

"Father, thank you for the letters. Thank you for nudging me to find the letter writers. I understand your presence and your grace more deeply now. Before, I felt emptiness and seemed to be wandering aimlessly and searching for something I couldn't identify. My efforts only disappointed me. This journey revealed the truth of my search. I'd never found what I was looking for because I never cast my eyes upon you, Father. I cried out for your presence to be in my life again, but I was too busy searching to stop and listen to you speak to me. I couldn't appreciate the beauty surrounding me and doors you opened for me because I was too focused on doing it myself.

"Father, for too many years I took my eyes away from you and got lost in the busyness of life and outward temptations. Thanks to these letters, I realize you were never far away and even when I didn't seek your presence, you found me. In the quietness of the beach house, I heard you again. In the letters, I saw my need for you. Listening to the stories, I learned to trust your healing presence. Their stories blessed me, and I realize how the worst circumstance and troubled times can become a testimony for others. Faith was right—beauty from ashes.

"Most important, Father, you taught me, that for you, *I am enough*, and if I turn to you, you will show me the peace we find when we put our faith and trust in you. Thank you for pursuing me with such a relentless love. And thank you so much for Faith, who constantly shows me what faith in you looks like. I cherish her friendship."

I looked at Faith, but before she could speak, I said, "Your friendship is one I often feel I don't deserve, but it's one I know I couldn't live without. You may not be my sister by birth, but you are my sister in Christ. You have never given up on me, even when you should have. Your faith in our Father and your love for me keeps me going. I am eternally grateful you're part of my life." I reached across the table and took her hand.

We were both overcome with emotion. Through our tears, we thanked each other for being everything the other needed in good times and in bad. Our friendship had endured many trials and tribulations, and we had watched each other grow into the persons our Father had meant for us to become.

Faith wiped the tears from her eyes and said, "Now we both know love in its purest form—the love from our Father. I believe he would say the answer to our letters is 1 John 4:16. Do you know the verse? 'And so we know and rely on the love God has for us. God is love. Whoever lives in love lives in God, and God in them.'"

I agreed with Faith, and as we stood to leave, I gave her a hug. "I also believe he is here right now," I told my best friend. "His eyes are filled with love, and his heart is saying, 'Well done, daughters; well done.'"

About the Author

Crissie Ann Leonard is an accounting associate at a nonprofit firm. A self-taught financial wiz, she has loved literature since she could read. Building on that love and personal experiences, she has spent the last decade writing novels based on life, faith, growth, and healing.

She has been a lifelong writer and first began with short stories and poetry, only to be sidetracked by life—joy and sorrow, love and loss.

She lives in Ohio with her family. Her great loves are God; her cat, Smokey; her family; and Chewbacca from *Star Wars*. When God's purpose rose to meet her pain, this book was born.

CPSIA information can be obtained
at www.ICGtesting.com
Printed in the USA
BVHW030332101019
560726BV00029B/28/P